The Consolidator

or,
Memoirs of Sundry Transactions
From the World in the Moon.

Translated from the Lunar Language,
By the Author of The True-born English Man.

Daniel Defoe

The Consolidator

Daniel Defoe

PO Box 2211
Fairfield, IA 52556
www.1stworldlibrary.org
First Edition

LCCN: 2004091174

Softcover ISBN: 1-59540-620-4
Hardcover ISBN: 1-4218-0920-6
eBook ISBN: 1-59540-720-0

The Consolidator

contributed by the Charles Family
in support of
1st World Library Literary Society

The Consolidator

It cannot be unknown to any that have travell'd into the Dominions of the Czar of Muscovy, that this famous rising Monarch, having studied all Methods for the Encrease of his Power, and the Enriching as well as Polishing his Subjects, has travell'd through most part of Europe, and visited the Courts of the greatest Princes; from whence, by his own Observation, as well as by carrying with him Artists in most useful Knowledge, he has transmitted most of our General Practice, especially in War and Trade, to his own Unpolite People; and the Effects of this Curiosity of his are exceeding visible in his present Proceedings; for by the Improvements he obtained in his European Travels, he has Modell'd his Armies, form'd new Fleets, settled Foreign Negoce in several remote Parts of the World; and we now see his Forces besieging strong Towns, with regular Approaches; and his Engineers raising Batteries, throwing Bombs, &c. like other Nations; whereas before, they had nothing of Order among them, but carried all by Ouslaught and Scalado, wherein they either prevailed by the Force of Irresistible Multitude, or were Slaughter'd by heaps, and left the Ditches of their Enemies fill'd with their Dead Bodies.

We see their Armies now form'd into regular Battalions; and their Strelitz Musqueteers, a People equivalent to the Turks Janizaries, cloath'd like our Guards, firing in Platoons, and behaving themselves with extraordinary Bravery and Order.

We see their Ships now compleatly fitted, built and furnish'd, by the English and Dutch Artists, and their Men of War Cruize in the Baltick. Their New City of Petersburgh built by the present Czar, begins now to look like our Portsmouth, fitted with Wet and Dry Docks, Storehouses, and Magazines of Naval Preparations, vast and Incredible; which may serve to remind us, how we once taught the French to build Ships, till they are grown able to teach us how to use them.

As to Trade, our large Fleets to Arch-Angel may speak for it, where we now send 100 Sail yearly, instead of 8 or 9, which were the greatest number we ever sent before; and the Importation of Tobaccoes from England into his Dominions, would still increase the Trade thither, was not the Covetousness of our own Merchants the Obstruction of their Advantages. But all this by the by.

As this great Monarch has Improved his Country, by introducing the Manners and Customs of the Politer Nations of Europe; so, with Indefatigable Industry, he has settled a new, but constant Trade, between his Country and China, by Land; where his Carravans go twice or thrice a Year, as Numerous almost, and as strong, as those from Egypt to Persia: Nor is the Way shorter, or the Desarts they pass over less wild and uninhabitable, only that they are not so subject to Flouds of Sand, if that Term be proper, or to Troops of Arabs, to destroy them by the way; for this powerful Prince, to make this terrible Journey feazible to his

Subjects, has built Forts, planted Collonies and Garisons at proper Distances; where, though they are seated in Countries intirely Barren, and among uninhabited Rocks and Sands; yet, by his continual furnishing them from his own Stores, the Merchants travelling are reliev'd on good Terms, and meet both with Convoy and Refreshment.

More might be said of the admirable Decorations of this Journey, and how so prodigious an Attempt is made easy; so that now they have an exact Correspondence, and drive a prodigious Trade between Muscow and Tonquin; but having a longer Voyage in Hand, I shall not detain the Reader, nor keep him till he grows too big with Expectation.

Now, as all Men know the Chineses are an Ancient, Wise, Polite, and most Ingenious People; so the Muscovites begun to reap the Benefit of this open Trade; and not only to grow exceeding Rich by the bartering for all the Wealth of those Eastern Countries; but to polish and refine their Customs and Manners, as much on that side as they have from their European Improvements on this.

And as the Chineses have many sorts of Learning which these Parts of the World never heard of, so all those useful Inventions which we admire ourselves so much for, are vulgar and common with them, and were in use long before our Parts of the World were Inhabited. Thus Gun-powder, Printing, and the use of the Magnet and Compass, which we call Modern Inventions, are not only far from being Inventions, but fall so far short of the Perfection of Art they have attained to, that it is hardly Credible, what wonderful things we are told of from thence, and all the Voyages the Author has made thither being imploy'd another way, have not yet furnish'd him with the Particulars fully enough to transmit them to view; not but that he is preparing a Scheme of all those excellent Arts those Nations are Masters of, for publick View, by way of Detection of the monstrous Ignorance and Deficiencies of European Science; which may serve as a Lexicon Technicum for this present Age, with useful Diagrams for that purpose; wherein I shall not fail to acqaint the World, 1. With the Art of Gunnery, as Practis'd in China long before the War of the Giants, and by which those Presumptuous Animals fired Red-hot Bullets right up into Heaven, and made a Breach sufficient to encourage them to a General Storm; but being Repulsed with great Slaughter, they gave over the Siege for that time. This memorable part of History shall be a faithful Abridgement of Ibra chizra-le-peglizar, Historiagrapher-Royal to the Emperor of China, who wrote Anno Mundi 114. his Volumes extant, in the Publick Library at Tonquin, Printed in Leaves of Vitrify'd Diamond, by an admirable Dexterity, struck all at an oblique Motion, the Engine remaining intire, and still fit for use, in the Chamber of the Emperor's Rarities.

And here I shall give you a Draft of the Engine it self, and a Plan of its Operation, and the wonderful Dexterity of its Performance.

If these Labours of mine shall prove successful, I may in my next Journey that way, take an Abstract of their most admirable Tracts in Navigation, and the Mysteries of Chinese Mathematicks; which out-do all Modern Invention at that Rate, that 'tis Inconceivable: In this Elaborate Work I must run thro' the 365 Volumes of Augro-machi-lanquaro-zi, the most ancient Mathematician in all China: From thence I shall give a Description of a Fleet of Ships of 100000 Sail, built at the Expence of the Emperor Tangro the 15th; who having Notice of the General Deluge, prepar'd these Vessels, to every City and Town in his Dominions One, and in Bulk proportion'd to the number of its Inhabitants; into which Vessel all the People, with such Moveables as they thought fit to save, and with 120 Days Provisions, were receiv'd at the time of the Floud; and the rest of their Goods being put into great Vessels made of China Ware, and fast luted down on the top, were preserv'd unhurt by the Water: These Ships they furnish'd with 600 Fathom of Chain instead of Cables; which being fastned by wonderful Arts to the Earth, every Vessel rid out the Deluge just at the Town's end; so that when the Waters abated, the People had nothing to do, but to open the Doors made in the Ship-sides, and come out, repair their Houses, open the great China Pots their Goods were in, and so put themselves in Statu Quo.

The Draft of one of these Ships I may perhaps obtain by my Interest in the present Emperor's Court, as it has been preserv'd ever since, and constantly repair'd, riding at Anchor in a great Lake, about 100 Miles from Tonquin; in which all the People of that City were preferv'd, amounting by their Computation to about a Million and half.

And as these things must be very useful in these Parts, to abate the Pride and Arrogance of our Modern Undertakers of great Enterprizes, Authors of strange Foreign Accounts, Philosophical Transactions, and the like; if Time and Opportunity permit, I may let them know, how Infinitely we are out-done by those refined Nations, in all manner of Mechanick Improvements and Arts; and in discoursing of this, it will necessarily come in my way to speak of a most Noble Invention, being an Engine I would recommend to all People to whom 'tis necessary to have a good Memory; and which I design, if possible, to obtain a Draft of, that it may be Erected in our Royal Societies Laboratory: It has the wonderfullest Operations in the World: One part of it furnishes a Man of Business to dispatch his Affairs strangely; for if he be a Merchant, he shall write his Letters with one Hand, and Copy them with the other; if he is posting his Books, he shall post the Debtor side with one Hand, and the Creditor with the other; if he be a Lawyer, he draws his Drafts with one Hand, and Ingrosses them with the other.

Another part of it furnishes him with such an Expeditious way of Writing, or Transcribing, that a Man cannot speak so fast, but he that hears shall have it down in Writing before 'tis spoken; and a Preacher shall deliver himself to his Auditory, and having this Engine before him, shall put down every thing he says in Writing at the same time; and so exactly is this Engine squar'd by Lines and Rules, that it does not require him that Writes to keep his Eye upon it.

I am told, in some Parts of China, they had arriv'd to such a Perfection of Knowledge, as to understand one anothers Thoughts; and that it was found to be an excellent Preservative to humane Society, against all sorts of Frauds, Cheats, Sharping, and many Thousand European Inventions of that Nature, at which only we can be said to out-do those Nations.

I confess, I have not yet had leisure to travel those Parts, having been diverted by an accidental Opportunity of a new Voyage I had occasion to make for farther Discoveries, and which the Pleasure and Usefulness thereof having been very great, I have omitted the other for the present, but shall not fail to make a Visit to those Parts the first Opportunity, and shall give my Country-men the best Account I can of those things; for I doubt not in Time to bring our Nation, so fam'd for improving other People's Discoveries, to be as wise as any of those Heathen Nations; I wish I had the same Prospect of making them half so honest.

I had spent but a few Months in this Country, but my search after the Prodigy of humane Knowledge the People abounds with, led me into Acquaintance with some of their principal Artists, Engineers, and Men of Letters; and I was astonish'd at every Day's Discovery of new and of unheard-of Worlds of Learning; but I Improv'd in the Superficial Knowledge of their General, by no body so much as by my Conversation with the Library-keeper of Tonquin, by whom I had Admission into the vast Collection of Books, which the Emperors of that Country have treasur'd up.

It would be endless to give you a Catalogue, and they admit of no Strangers to write any thing down, but what the Memory can retain, you are welcome to carry away with you; and amongst the wonderful Volumes of Antient and Modern Learning, I could not but take Notice of a few; which, besides those I mentioned before, I saw, when I lookt over this vast Collection; and a larger Account may be given in our next.

It would be needless to Transcribe the Chinese Character, or to put their Alphabet into our Letters, because the Words would be both Unintelligible, and very hard to Pronounce; and therefore, to avoid hard

Words, and Hyroglyphicks, I'll translate them as well as I can.

The first Class I came to of Books, was the Constitutions of the Empire; these are vast great Volumes, and have a sort of Engine like our Magna Charta, to remove 'em, and with placing them in a Frame, by turning a Screw, open'd the Leaves, and folded them this way, or that, as the Reader desires. It was present Death for the Library-keeper to refuse the meanest Chinese Subject to come in and read them; for 'tis their Maxim, That all People ought to know the Laws by which they are to be govern'd; and as above all People, we find no Fools in this Country, so the Emperors, though they seem to be Arbitrary, enjoy the greatest Authority in the World, by always observing, with the greatest Exactness, the Pacta Conventa of their Government: From these Principles it is impossible we should ever hear, either of the Tyranny of Princes, or Rebellion of Subjects, in all their Histories.

At the Entrance into this Class, you find some Ancient Comments, upon the Constitution of the Empire, written many Ages before we pretend the World began; but above all, One I took particular notice of, which might bear this Title, Natural Right prov'd Superior to Temporal Power; wherein the old Author proves, the Chinese Emperors were Originally made so, by Nature's directing the People, to place the Power of Government in the most worthy Person they could find; and the Author giving a most exact History of 2000 Emperors, brings them into about 35 or 36 Periods of Lines when the Race ended; and when a Collective Assembly of the Nobles, Cities, and People, Nominated a new Family to the Goverment.

This being an heretical Book as to European Politicks, and our Learned Authors having long since exploded this Doctrine, and prov'd that Kings and Emperors came down from Heaven with Crowns on their Heads, and all their Subjects were born with Saddles on their Backs; I thought fit to leave it where I found it, least our excellent Tracts of Sir Robert Filmer, Dr. Hammond L...y, S....l, and Others, who have so learnedly treated of the more useful Doctrine of Passive Obedience, Divine Right, &c. should be blasphem'd by the Mob, grow into Contempt of the People; and they should take upon them to question their Superiors for the Blood of Algernon Sidney, and Argyle.

For I take the Doctrines of Passive Obedience, &c. among the States-men, to be like the Copernican System of the Earths Motion among Philosophers; which, though it be contrary to all antient Knowledge, and not capable of Demonstration, yet is adher'd to in general, because by this they can better solve, and give a more rational Account of several dark Phanomena in Nature, than they could before.

Thus our Modern States-men approve of this Scheme of Government; not that it admits of any rational Defence, much less of Demonstration, but because by this Method they can the better explain, as well as defend, all Coertion in Cases invasive of Natural Right, than they could before.

Here I found two famous Volumes in Chyrurgery, being an exact Description of the Circulation of the Blood, discovered long before King Solomon's Allegory of the Bucket's going to the Well; with several curious Methods by which the Demonstration was to be made so plain, as would make even the worthy Doctor B - himself become a Convert to his own Eye-sight, make him damn his own Elaborate Book, and think it worse Nonsence than ever the Town had the Freedom to imagine.

All our Philosophers are Fools, and their Transactions a parcel of empty Stuff, to the Experiments of the Royal Societies in this Country. Here I came to a Learned Tract of Winds, which outdoes even the Sacred Text, and would make us believe it was not wrote to those People; for they tell Folks whence it comes, and whither it goes. There you have an Account how to make Glasses of Hogs Eyes, that can see the Wind; and they give strange Accounts both of its regular and irregular Motions, its Compositions and Quantities; from whence, by a sort of Algebra, they can cast up its Duration, Violence, and Extent: In these Calculations, some say, those Authors have been so exact, that they can, as our Philosophers say of Comets, state their Revolutions, and tell us how many Storms there shall happen to any Period of time, and when; and perhaps this may be with much about the same Truth.

It was a certain Sign Aristotle had never been at China; for, had he seen the 216th Volume of the Chinese Navigation, in the Library I am speaking of, a large Book in Double Folio, wrote by the Famous Mira-cho-cho-lasmo, Vice-Admiral of China, and said to be printed there about 2000 Years before the Deluge, in the Chapter of Tides he would have seen the Reason of all the certain and uncertain Fluxes and Refluxes of that Element, how the exact Pace is kept between the Moon and the Tides, with a most elaborate Discourse there, of the Power of Sympathy, and the manner how the heavenly Bodies Influence the Earthly: Had he seen this, the Stagyrite would never have Drowned himself, because he could not comprehend this Mystery.

'Tis farther related of this Famous Author, that he was no Native of this World, but was Born in the Moon, and coming hither to make Discoveries, by a strange Invention arrived to by the Virtuosoes of that habitable World, the Emperor of China prevailed with him to stay and improve his Subjects, in the most exquisite Accomplishments of those Lunar Regions; and no wonder the Chinese are such exquisite Artists, and Masters of such sublime Knowledge, when this Famous Author has blest them with such unaccountable Methods of Improvement.

There was abundance of vast Classes full of the Works of this wonderful Philosopher: He gave the how, the modus of all the secret Operations of Nature; and told us, how Sensation is convey'd to and from the Brain; why Respiration preserves Life; and how Locomotion is directed to, as well as perform'd by the Parts. There are some Anatomical Dissections of Thought, and a Mathematical Description of Nature's strong Box, the Memory, with all its Locks and Keys.

There you have that part of the Head turn'd in-side outward, in which Nature has placed the Materials of reflecting; and like a Glass Bee-hive, represents to you all the several Cells in which are lodg'd things past, even back to Infancy and Conception. There you have the Repository, with all its Cells, Classically, Annually, Numerically, and Alphabetically Dispos'd. There you may see how, when the perplext Animal, on the loss of a Thought or Word, scratches his Pole:

Every Attack of his Invading Fingers knocks at Nature's Door, allarms all the Register-keepers, and away they run, unlock all the Classes, search diligently for what he calls for, and immediately deliver it up to the Brain; if it cannot be found, they intreat a little Patience, till they step into the Revolvary, where they run over little Catalogues of the minutest Passages of Life, and so in time never fail to hand on the thing; if not just when he calls for it, yet at some other time.

And thus, when a thing lyes very Abstruse, and all the rumaging of the whole House cannot find it; nay, when all the People in the House have given it over, they very often find one thing when they are looking for another.

Next you have the Retentive in the remotest part of the Place, which, like the Records in the Tower, takes Possession of all Matters, as they are removed from the Classes in the Repository, for want of room. These are carefully Lockt, and kept safe, never to be open'd but upon solemn Occasions, and have swinging great Bars and Bolts upon them; so that what is kept here, is seldom lost. Here Conscience has one large Ware-house, and the Devil another; the first is very seldom open'd, but has a Chink or Till, where all the Follies and Crimes of Life being minuted are dropt in; but as the Man seldom cares to look in, the Locks are very Rusty, and not open'd but with great Difficulty, and on extraordinary Occasions, as Sickness, Afflictions, Jails, Casualties, and Death; and then the Bars all give way at once; and being prest from within with a more than ordinary Weight, burst as a Cask of Wine upon the Fret, which for want of Vent, makes all the Hoops fly.

As for the Devil's Ware-house, he has two constant

Warehouse-keepers, Pride and Conceit, and these are always at the Door, showing their Wares, and exposing the pretended Vertues and Accomplishments of the Man, by way of Ostentation.

In the middle of this curious part of Nature, there is a clear Thorough-fare, representing the World, through which so many Thousand People pass so easily, and do so little worth taking notice of, that 'tis for no manner of Signification to leave Word they have been here. Thro' this Opening pass Millions of things not worth remembring, and which the Register-Keepers, who stand at the Doors of the Classes, as they go by, take no notice of; such as Friendships, helps in Distress, Kindnesses in Affliction, Voluntary Services, and all sorts of Importunate Merit; things which being but Trifles in their own Nature, are made to be forgotten.

In another Angle is to be seen the Memory's Garden, in which her most pleasant things are not only Deposited, but Planted, Transplanted, Grafted, Inoculated, and obtain all possible Propagation and Encrease; these are the most pleasant, delightful, and agreeable things, call'd Envy, Slander, Revenge, Strife and Malice, with the Additions of Ill-turns, Reproaches, and all manner of Wrong; these are caressed in the Cabinet of the Memory, with a World of Pleasure never let pass, and carefully Cultivated with all imaginable Art.

There are multitudes of Weeds, Toys, Chat, Story, Fiction, and Lying, which in the great throng of passant Affairs, stop by the way, and crowding up the Place, leave no room for their Betters that come behind, which makes many a good Guess be put by, and left to go clear thro' for want of Entertainment.

There are a multitude of things very curious and observable, concerning this little, but very accurate thing, called Memory; but above all, I see nothing so very curious, as the wonderful Art of Wilful Forgetfulness; and as 'tis a thing, indeed, I never could find any Person compleatly Master of, it pleased me very much, to find this Author has made a large Essay, to prove there is really no such Power in Nature; and that the Pretenders to it are all Impostors, and put a Banter upon the World; for that it is impossible for any Man to oblige himself to forget a thing, since he that can remember to forget, and at the same time forget to remember, has an Art above the Devil.

In his Laboratory you see a Fancy preserv'd a la Mummy, several Thousand Years old; by examining which you may perfectly discern, how Nature makes a Poet: Another you have taken from a meer Natural, which discovers the Reasons of Nature's Negative in the Case of humane Understanding; what Deprivation of Parts She suffers, in the Composition of a Coxcomb; and with what wonderful Art She prepares a Man to be a Fool.

Here being the product of this Author's wonderful Skill, you have the Skeleton of a Wit, with all the Readings of Philosophy and Chyrurgery upon the Parts: Here you see all the Lines Nature has drawn to form a Genius, how it performs, and from what Principles.

Also you are Instructed to know the true reason of the Affinity between Poetry and Poverty; and that it is equally derived from what's Natural and Intrinsick, as from Accident and Circumstance; how the World being always full of Fools and Knaves, Wit is sure to miss of a good Market; especially, if Wit and Truth happen to come in Company; for the Fools don't understand it, and the Knaves can't bear it.

But still 'tis own'd, and is most apparent, there is something also Natural in the Case too, since there are some particular Vessels Nature thinks necessary, to the more exact Composition of this nice thing call'd a Wit, which as they are, or are not Interrupted in the peculiar Offices for which they are appointed, are subject to various Distempers, and more particularly to Effluxions and Vapour, Diliriums Giddiness of the Brain, and Lapsa, or Looseness of the Tongue; and as these Distempers, occasion'd by the exceeding quantity of Volatiles, Nature is obliged to make use of in the Composition, are hardly to be avoided, the Disasters which generally they push the Animal into, are as necessarily consequent to them as Night is to the Setting of the Sun; and these are very many, as disobliging Parents, who have frequently in this Country whipt their Sons for making Verses; and here I could not but reflect how useful a Discipline early Correction must be to a Poet; and how easy the Town had been had N - t, E - w, T. B - P - s, D - S - D - fy, and an Hundred more of the jingling Train of our modern Rhymers, been Whipt young, very young, for Poetasting, they had never perhaps suckt in that Venome of Ribaldry, which all the Satyr of the Age has never been able to scourge out of them to this Day.

The further fatal Consequences of these unhappy Defects in Nature, where she has damn'd a Man to Wit and Rhyme, has been loss of Inheritance, Parents being aggravated by the obstinate young Beaus, resolving to be Wits in spight of Nature, the wiser Head has been obliged to Confederate with Nature, and with-hold the

Birth-right of Brains, which otherwise the young Gentleman might have enjoy'd, to the great support of his Family and Posterity. Thus the famous Waller, Denham, Dryden, and sundry Others, were oblig'd to condemn their Race to Lunacy and Blockheadism, only to prevent the fatal Destruction of their Families, and entailing the Plague of Wit and Weathercocks upon their Posterity.

The yet farther Extravagancies which naturally attend the Mischief of Wit, are Beau-ism, Dogmaticality, Whimsification, Impudensity, and various kinds of Fopperosities (according to Mr. Boyl,) which issuing out of the Brain, descend into all the Faculties, and branch themselves by infinite Variety, into all the Actions of Life.

These by Conseqence, Beggar the Head, the Tail, the Purse, and the whole Man, till he becomes as poor and despicable as Negative Nature can leave him, abandon'd of his Sense, his Manners, his Modesty, and what's worse, his Money, having nothing left but his Poetry, dies in a Ditch, or a Garret, A-la-mode de Tom Brown, uttering Rhymes and Nonsence to the last Moment.

In Pity to all my unhappy Brethren, who suffer under these Inconveniencies, I cannot but leave it on Record, that they may not be reproached with being Agents of their own Misfortunes, since I assure them, Nature has form'd them with the very Necessity of acting like Coxcombs, fixt upon them by the force of Organick Consequences, and placed down at the very Original Effusion of that fatal thing call'd Wit.

Nor is the Discovery less wonderful than edifying, and

no humane Art on our side the World ever found out such a Sympathetick Influence, between the Extreams of Wit and Folly, till this great Lunarian Naturalist furnisht us with such unheard-of Demonstrations.

Nor is this all I learnt from him, tho' I cannot part with this, till I have publisht a Memento Mori, and told 'em what I had discovered of Nature in these remote Parts of the World, from whence I take the Freedom to tell these Gentlemen, That if they please to Travel to these distant Parts, and examine this great Master of Nature's Secrets, they may every Man see what cross Strokes Nature has struck, to finish and form every extravagant Species of that Heterogenious Kind we call Wit.

There C - S - may be inform'd how he comes to be very Witty, and a Mad-man all at once; and P - r may see, That with less Brains and more P - x he is more a Wit and more a Mad-man than the Coll. Ad - son may tell his Master my Lord - the reason from Nature, why he would not take the Court's Word, nor write the Poem call'd, The Campaign, till he had 200 l. per Annum secur'd to him; since 'tis known they have but one Author in the Nation that writes for 'em for nothing, and he is labouring very hard to obtain the Title of Blockhead, and not be paid for it: Here D. might understand, how he came to be able to banter all Mankind, and yet all Mankind be able to banter him; at the fame time our numerous throng of Parnassians may see Reasons for the variety of the Negative and Positive Blessings they enjoy; some for having Wit and no Verse, some Verse and no Wit, some Mirth without Jest, some Jest without Fore-cast, some Rhyme and no Jingle, some all Jingle and no Rhyme, some Language without measure; some all Quantity and no Cudence, some all Wit and no Sence, some all Sence and no Flame, some Preach in Rhyme, some sing when they Preach, some all Song and no Tune, some all Tune and no Song; all these Unaccountables have their Originals, and can be answer'd for in unerring Nature, tho' in our out-side Guesses we can say little to it. Here is to be seen, why some are all Nature, some all Art; some beat Verse out of the Twenty-four rough Letters, with Ten Hammers and Anvils to every Line, and maul the Language as a Swede beats Stock-Fish; Others buff Nature, and bully her out of whole Stanza's of ready-made Lines at a time, carry all before them, and rumble like distant Thunder in a black Cloud: Thus Degrees and Capacities are fitted by Nature, according to Organick Efficacy; and the Reason and Nature of Things are found in themselves: Had D - y seen his own Draft by this Light of Chinese Knowledge, he might have known he should be a Coxcomb without writing Twenty-two Plays, to stand as so many Records against him. Dryden might have told his Fate, that having his extraordinary Genius flung and pitcht upon a Swivle, it would certainly turn round as fast as the Times, and instruct him how to write Elegies to O. C. and King C. the Second, with all the Coherence imaginable; how to write Religio Laicy, and the Hind and Panther, and yet be the same Man, every Day to change his Principle, change his Religion, change his Coat, change his Master, and yet never change his Nature.

There are abundance of other Secrets in Nature discover'd in relation to these things, too many to repeat, and yet too useful to omit, as the reason why Phisicians are generally Atheists; and why Atheists are universally Fools, and generally live to know it themselves, the real Obstructions, which prevent fools being mad, all the Natural Causes of Love, abundance of Demonstrations of the Synonimous Nature of Love and Leachery, especially consider'd a la Modern, with an absolute Specifick for the Frenzy of Love, found out in the Constitution, Anglice, a Halter.

It would be endless to reckon up the numerous Improvements, and wonderful Discoveries this extraordinary Person has brought down, and which are to be seen in his curious Chamber of Rarities.

Particularly, a Map of Parnassus, with an exact Delineation of all the Cells, Apartments, Palaces and Dungeons, of that most famous Mountain; with a Description of its Heighth, and a learned Dissertation, proving it to be the properest Place next to the P - e House to take a Rise at, for a flight to the World in the Moon.

Also some Enquiries, whether Noah's Ark did not first rest upon it; and this might be one of the Summits of Ararat, with some Confutations of the gross and palpable Errors, which place this extraordinary Skill among the Mountains of the Moon in Africa.

Also you have here a Muse calcin'd, a little of the Powder of which given to a Woman big with Child, if it be a Boy it will be a Poet, if a Girl she'll be a Whore, if an Hermaphrodite it will be Lunatick.

Strange things, they tell us, have been done with this calcin'd Womb of Imagination; if the Body it came from was a Lyrick Poet, the Child will be a Beau, or a Beauty; if an Heroick Poet, he will be a Bulley; if his Talent was Satyr, he'll be a Philosopher.

Another Muse they tell us, they have dissolv'd into a

Liquid, and kept with wondrous Art, the Vertues of which are Soveraign against Ideotism, Dullness, and all sorts of Lethargick Diseases; but if given in too great a quantity, creates Poesy, Poverty, Lunacy, and the Devil in the Head ever after.

I confess, I always thought these Muses strange intoxicating things, and have heard much talk of their Original, but never was acquainted with their Vertue a la Simple before; however, I would always advise People against too large a Dose of Wit, and think the Physician must be a Mad-man that will venture to prescribe it.

As all these noble Acquirements came down with this wonderful Man from the World in the Moon, it furnisht me with these useful Observations.

1. That Country must needs be a Place of strange Perfection, in all parts of extraordinary Knowledge.

2. How useful a thing it would be for most sorts of our People, especially Statesmen, P - t-men, Convocation-men, Phylosophers, Physicians, Quacks, Mountebanks, Stock-jobbers, and all the Mob of the Nation's Civil or Ecclesiastical Bone-setters, together with some Men of the Law, some of the Sword, and all of the Pen: I say, how useful and improving a thing it must be to them, to take a Journey up to the World in the Moon; but above all, how much more beneficial it would be to them that stay'd behind.

3. That it is not to be wonder'd at, why the Chinese excell so much all these Parts of the World, since but for that Knowledge which comes down to them from the World in the Moon, they would be like

other People.

4. No Man need to Wonder at my exceeding desire to go up to the World in the Moon, having heard of such extraordinary Knowledge to be obtained there, since in the search of Knowledge and Truth, wiser Men than I have taken as unwarrantable Flights, and gone a great deal higher than the Moon, into a strange Abbyss of dark Phanomena, which they neither could make other People understand, nor ever rightly understood themselves, witness Malbranch, Mr. Lock, Hobbs, the Honourable Boyle and a great many others, besides Messieurs Norris, Asgil, Coward, and the Tale of a Tub.

This great Searcher into Nature has, besides all this, left wonderful Discoveries and Experiments behind him; but I was with nothing more exceedingly diverted, than with his various Engines, and curious Contrivances, to go to and from his own Native Country the Moon. All our Mechanick Motions of Bishop Wilkins, or the artificial Wings of the Learned Spaniard, who could have taught God Almighty how to have mended the Creation, are Fools to this Gentleman; and because no Man in China has made more Voyages up into the Moon than my self, I cannot but give you some Account of the easyness of the Passage, as well as of the Country.

Nor are his wonderful Tellescopes of a mean Quality, by which such plain Discoveries are made, of the Lands and Seas in the Moon, and in all the habitable Planets, that one may as plainly fee what a Clock it is by one of the Dials in the Moon, as if it were no farther off than Windsor-Castle; and had he liv'd to finish the Speaking-trumpet which he had contriv'd to convey

Sound thither, Harlequin's Mock-Trumpet had been a Fool to it; and it had no doubt been an admirable Experiment, to have given us a general Advantage from all their acquir'd Knowledge in those Regions, where no doubt several useful Discoveries are daily made by the Men of Thought for the Improvement of all sorts of humane Understanding, and to have discoursed with them on those things, must have been very pleasant, besides, its being very much to our particular Advantage.

I confess, I have thought it might have been very useful to this Nation, to have brought so wonderful an Invention hither, and I was once very desirous to have set up my rest here, and for the Benefit of my Native Country, have made my self Master of these Engines, that I might in due time have convey'd them to our Royal Society, that once in 40 Years they might have been said to do something for Publick Good; and that the Reputation and Usefulness of the so so's might be recover'd in England; but being told that in the Moon there were many of these Glasses to be had very cheap, and I having declar'd my Resolution of undertaking a Voyage thither, I deferred my Design, and shall defer my treating of them, till I give some Account of my Arrival there.

But above all his Inventions for making this Voyage, I saw none more pleasant or profitable, than a certain Engine formed in the shape of a Chariot, on the Backs of two vast Bodies with extended Wings, which spread about 50 Yards in Breadth, compos'd of Feathers so nicely put together, that no Air could pass; and as the Bodies were made of Lunar Earth which would bear the Fire, the Cavities were fill'd with an Ambient Flame, which fed on a certain Spirit deposited in a proper quantity, to last out the Voyage; and this Fire so order'd as to move about such Springs and Wheels as kept the Wings in a most exact and regular Motion, always ascendant; thus the Person being placed in this airy Chariot, drinks a certain dozing Draught, that throws him into a gentle Slumber, and Dreaming all the way, never wakes till he comes to his Journey's end.

Of the Consolidator.

These Engines are call'd in their Country Language, Dupekasses; and according to the Ancient Chinese, or Tartarian, Apezolanthukanistes; in English, a Consolidator.

The Composition of this Engine is very admirable; for, as is before noted, 'tis all made up of Feathers, and the quality of the Feathers, is no less wonderful than their Composition; and therefore, I hope the Reader will bear with the Description for the sake of the Novelty, since I assure him such things as these are not to be seen in every Country.

The number of Feathers are just 513, they are all of a length and breadth exactly, which is absolutely necessary to the floating Figure, or else one side or any one part being wider or longer than the rest, it would interrupt the motion of the whole Engine; only there is one extraordinary Feather which, as there is an odd one in the number, is placed in the Center, and is the Handle, or rather Rudder to the whole Machine: This Feather is every way larger than its Fellows, 'tis almost as long and broad again; but above all, its Quill or Head is much larger, and it has as it were several small bushing Feathers round the bottom of it, which all make but one presiding or superintendent Feather, to guide, regulate, and pilot the whole Body.

Nor are these common Feathers, but they are pickt and cull'd out of all parts of the Lunar Country, by the Command of the Prince; and every Province sends up the best they can find, or ought to do so at least, or else they are very much to blame; for the Employment they are put to being of so great use to the Publick, and the Voyage or Flight so exceeding high, it would be very ill done if, when the King sends his Letters about the Nation, to pick him up the best Feathers they can lay their Hands on, they should send weak, decay'd, or half-grown Feathers, and yet sometimes it happens so; and once there was such rotten Feathers collected, whether it was a bad Year for Feathers, or whether the People that gather'd them had a mind to abuse their King; but the Feathers were so bad, the Engine was good for nothing, but broke before it was got half way; and by a double Misfortune, this happen'd to be at an unlucky time, when the King himself had resolv'd on a Voyage, or Flight to to the Moon; but being deceiv'd, by the unhappy Miscarriage of the deficient Feathers, he fell down from so great a height, that he struck himself against his own Palace, and beat his Head off.

Nor had the Sons of this Prince much better Success, tho' the first of them was a Prince mightily belov'd by his Subjects; but his Misfortunes chiefly proceeded from his having made use of one of the Engines so very long, that the Feathers were quite worn out, and good for nothing: He used to make a great many Voyages and Flights into the Moon, and then would make his Subjects give him great Sums of Money to come down to them again; and yet they were so fond of him, That they always complyed with him, and would give him every thing he askt, rather than to be without him: But they grew wiser since.

At last, this Prince used his Engine so long, it could hold together no longer; and being obliged to write to his Subjects to pick him out some new Feathers, they did so; but withall sent him such strong Feathers, and so stiff, that when he had placed 'em in their proper places, and made a very beautiful Engine, it was too heavy for him to manage: He made a great many Essays at it, and had it placed on the top of an old Idol Chappel, dedicated to an old Bramyn Saint of those Countries, called, Phantosteinaschap; in Latin, chap. de Saint Stephano; or in English, St. Stephen's: Here the Prince try'd all possible Contrivances, and a vast deal of Money it cost him; but the Feathers were so stiff they would not work, and the Fire within was so choaked and smother'd with its own Smoak, for want of due Vent and Circulation, that it would not burn; so he was oblig'd to take it down again; and from thence he carried it to his College of Bramyn Priests, and set it up in one of their Publick Buildings: There he drew Circles of Ethicks and Politicks, and fell to casting of Figures and Conjuring, but all would not do, the Feathers could not be brought to move; and, indeed, I have observ'd, That these Engines are seldom helpt by Art and Contrivance; there is no way with them, but to have the People spoke to, to get good Feathers; and they are easily placed, and perform all the several Motions with the greatest Ease and Accuracy imaginable; but it must be all Nature; any thing of Force distorts and dislocates them, and the whole Order is spoiled; and if there be but one Feather out of place, or pincht, or stands wrong, the D - l would not ride in the Chariot.

The Prince thus finding his Labour in vain, broke the Engine to pieces, and sent his Subjects Word what bad Feathers they had sent him: But the People, who knew it was his own want of Management, and that the Feathers were good enough, only a little stiff at first, and with good Usage would have been brought to be fit for use, took it ill, and never would send him any other as long as he liv'd: However, it had this good effect upon him, That he never made any more Voyages to the Moon as long as he reign'd.

His Brother succeeded him; and truly he was resolved upon a Voyage to the Moon, as soon as ever he came to the Crown. He had met with some unkind Usage from the Religious Lunesses of his own Country; and he turn'd Abogratziarian, a zealous fiery Sect something like our Anti-every-body-arians in England. 'Tis confest, some of the Bramyns of his Country were very false to him, put him upon several Ways of extending his Power over his Subjects, contrary to the Customs of the People, and contrary to his own Interest; and when the People expressed their Dislike of it, he thought to have been supported by those Clergy-men; but they failed him, and made good, that Old English Verse;

That Priests of all Religions are the same.

He took this so hainously, that he conceiv'd a just Hatred against those that had deceiv'd him; and as Resentments seldom keep Rules, unhappily entertain'd Prejudices against all the rest; and not finding it easy to bring all his Designs to pass better, he resolved upon a Voyage to the Moon.

Accordingly, he sends a Summons to all his People

according to Custom, to collect the usual quantity of Feathers for that purpose; and because he would be sure not be used as his Brother and Father had been, he took care to send certain Cunning-men Express, all over the Country, to bespeak the People's Care, in collecting, picking and culling them out, these were call'd in their Language, Tsopablesdetoo; which being Translated may signify in English, Men of Zeal, or Booted Apostles: Nor was this the only Caution this Prince used; for he took care, as the Feathers were sent up to him, to search and examine them one by one in his own Closet, to see if they were fit for his purpose; but, alas! he found himself in his Brother's Case exactly; and perceived, That his Subjects were generally disgusted at his former Conduct, about Abrogratzianism, and such things, and particularly set in a Flame by some of their Priests, call'd, Dullobardians, or Passive-Obedience-men, who had lately turn'd their Tale, and their Tail too upon their own Princes; and upon this, he laid aside any more Thoughts of the Engine, but took up a desperate and implacable Resolution, viz. to fly up to the Moon without it; in order to this, abundance of his Cunning-men were summon'd together to assist him, strange Engines contriv'd, and Methods propos'd; and a great many came from all Parts, to furnish him with Inventions and equivalent for their Journey; but all were so preposterous and ridiculous, that his Subjects seeing him going on to ruin himself, and by Consequence them too, unanimously took Arms; and if their Prince had not made his Escape into a foreign Country, 'tis thought they would have secur'd him for a Mad-man.

And here 'tis observable, That as it is in most such Cases, the mad Councellors of this Prince, when the

People begun to gather about him, fled; and every one shifted for themselves; nay, and some of them plunder'd him first of his Jewels and Treasure, and never were heard of since.

From this Prince none of the Kings or Government of that Country have ever seem'd to incline to the hazardous Attempt of the Voyage to the Moon, at least not in such a hair-brain'd manner.

However, the Engine has been very accurately Re-built and finish'd; and the People are now oblig'd by a Law, to send up new Feathers every three Years, to prevent the Mischiefs which happen'd by that Prince aforesaid, keeping one Set so long that it was dangerous to venture with them; and thus the Engine is preserved fit for use.

And yet has not this Engine been without its continual Disasters, and often out of repair; for though the Kings of the Country, as has been Noted, have done riding on the back of it, yet the restless Courtiers and Ministers of State have frequently obtained the Management of it, from the too easy Goodness of their Masters, or the Evils of the Times.

To Cure this, the Princes frequently chang'd Hands, turn'd one Set of Men out and put another in: But this made things still worse; for it divided the People into Parties and Factions in the State, and still the Strife was, who should ride in this Engine; and no sooner were these Skaet-Riders got into it, but they were for driving all the Nation up to the Moon: But of this by it self.

Authors differ concerning the Original of these

Feathers, and by what most exact Hand they were first appointed to this particular use; and as their Original is hard to be found, so it seems a Difficulty to resolve from what sort of Bird these Feathers are obtained: Some have nam'd one, some another; but the most Learned in those Climates call it by a hard Word, which the Printer having no Letters to express, and being in that place Hierogliphical, I can translate no better, than by the Name of a Collective: This must be a Strange Bird without doubt; it has Heads, Claws, Eyes and Teeth innumerable; and if I should go about to describe it to you, the History would be so Romantick, it would spoil the Credit of these more Authentick Relations which are yet behind.

'Tis sufficient, therefore, for the present, only to leave you this short Abridgement of the Story, as follows: This great Monstrous Bird, call'd the Collective, is very seldom seen, and indeed never, but upon Great Revolutions, and portending terrible Desolations and Destructions to a Country.

But he frequently sheds his Feathers; and they are carefully pickt up, by the Proprietors of those Lands where they fall; for none but those Proprietors may meddle with them; and they no sooner pick them up but they are sent to Court, where they obtain a new Name, and are called in a Word equally difficult to pronounce as the other, but Very like our English Word, Representative; and being placed in their proper Rows, with the Great Feather in the Center, and fitted for use, they lately obtained the Venerable Title of, The Consolidators; and the Machine it self, the Consolidator; and by that Name the Reader is desir'd for the future to let it be dignified and distinguish'd.

I cannot, however, forbear to descant a little here, on the Dignity and Beauty of these Feathers, being such as are hardly to be seen in any part of the World, but just in these remote Climates.

And First, Every Feather has various Colours, and according to the Variety of the Weather, are apt to look brighter and clearer, or paler and fainter, as the Sun happens to look on them with a stronger or weaker Aspect. The Quill or Head of every Feather is or ought to be full of a vigorous Substance, which gives Spirit, and supports the brightness and colour of the Feather; and as this is more or less in quantity, the bright Colour of the Feather is increased, or turns languid and pale.

Tis true, some of those Quills are exceeding empty and dry; and the Humid being totally exhal'd, those Feathers grow very useless and insignificant in a short time.

Some again are so full of Wind, and puft up with the Vapour of the Climate, that there's not Humid enough to Condence the Steam; and these are so fleet, so light, and so continually fluttering and troublesome, that they greatly serve to disturb and keep the Motion unsteddy.

Others either placed too near the inward concealed Fire, or the Head of the Quill being thin, the Fire causes too great a Fermentation; and the Consequence of this is so fatal, that sometimes it mounts the Engine up too fast, and indangers Precipitation: But 'tis happily observed, That these ill Feathers are but a very few, compar'd to the whole number; at the most, I never heard they were above 134 of the whole number: As for the empty ones, they are not very dangerous, but a sort of Good-for-nothing Feathers, that will fly when the greatest number of the rest fly, or stand still when they stand still. The fluttering hot-headed Feathers are the most dangerous, and frequently struggle hard to mount the Engine to extravagant heights; but still the greater number of the Feathers being stanch, and well fixt, as well as well furnisht, they always prevail, and check the Disorders the other would bring upon the Motion; so that upon the whole Matter, tho' there has sometims been oblique Motions, Variations, and sometimes great Wandrings out of the way, which may make the Passage tedious, yet it has always been a certain and safe Voyage; and no Engine was ever known to miscarry or overthrow, but that one mentioned before, and that was very much owing to the precipitate Methods the Prince took in guiding it; and tho' all the fault was laid in the Feathers, and they were to blame enough, yet I never heard any Wise Man, but what blam'd his Discretion, and particularly, a certain great Man has wrote three large Tracts of those Affairs, and call'd them, The History of the Opposition of the Feathers; wherein, tho' it was expected he would have curst the Engine it self and all the Feathers to the Devil, on the contrary, he lays equal blame on the Prince, who guided the Chariot with so unsteddy a hand, now as much too slack, as then too hard, turning them this way and that so hastily, that the Feathers could not move in their proper order; and this at last put the Fire in the Center quite out, and so the Engine over-set at once. This Impartiality has done great Justice to the Feathers, and set things in a clearer light: But of this I shall say more, when I come to treat of the Works of the Learned in this Lunar World.

This is hinted here only to inform the Reader, That this Engine is the safest Passage that ever was found out;

and that saving that one time, it never miscarried; nor if the common Order of things be observed, cannot Miscarry; for the good Feathers are always Negatives, when any precipitant Motion is felt, and immediately suppress it by their number; and these Negative Feathers are indeed the Travellers safety; the other are always upon the flutter, and upon every occasion hey for the Moon, up in the Clouds presently; but these Negative Feathers are never for going up, but when there is occasion for it; and from hence these fluttering fermented Feathers were called by the Antients High-flying Feathers, and the blustering things seem'd proud of the Name.

But to come to their general Character, the Feathers, speaking of them all together, are generally very Comely, Strong, Large, Beautiful things, their Quills or Heads well fixt, and the Cavities fill'd with a solid substantial Matter, which tho' it is full of Spirit, has a great deal of Temperament, and full of suitable well-dispos'd Powers, to the Operation for which they are design'd.

These placed, as I Noted before, in an extended Form like two great Wings, and operated by that sublime Flame; which being concealed in proper Receptacles, obtains its vent at the Cavities appointed, are supplied from thence with Life and Motion; and as Fire it fell, in the Opinion of some Learned Men, is nothing but Motion, and Motion tends to Fire: It can no more be a Wonder, if exalted in the Center of this famous Engine, a whole Nation should be carried up to the World in the Moon.

'Tis true, this Engine is frequently assaulted with fierce Winds, and furious Storms, which sometimes drive it a great way out of its way; and indeed, considering the length of the Passage, and the various Regions it goes through, it would be strange if it should meet with no Obstructions: These are oblique Gales, and cannot be said to blow from any of the Thirty-two Points, but Retrograde and Thwart: Some of these are call'd in their Language, Pensionazima, which is as much as to say, being Interpreted, a Court-breeze; another sort of Wind, which generally blows directly contrary to the Pensionazima, is the Clamorio, or in English, a Country Gale; this is generally Tempestuous, full of Gusts and Disgusts, Squauls and sudden Blasts, not without claps of Thunder, and not a little flashing of Heat and Party-fires.

There are a great many other Internal Blasts, which proceed from the Fire within, which sometimes not circulating right, breaks out in little Gusts of Wind and Heat, and is apt to indanger setting Fire to the Feathers, and this is more or less dangerous, according as among which of the Feathers it happens; for some of the Feathers are more apt to take Fire than others, as their Quills or Heads are more or less full of that solid Matter mention'd before.

The Engine suffers frequent Convulsions and Disorders from these several Winds; and which if they chance to overblow very much, hinder the Passage; but the Negative Feathers always apply Temper and Moderation; and this brings all to rights again.

For a Body like this, what can it not do? what cannot such an Extension perform in the Air? And when one thing is tackt to another, and properly Cosolidated into one mighty Consolidator, no question but whoever shall go up to the Moon, will find himself so improv'd in this wonderful Experiment, that not a Man ever perform'd that wonderful Flight, but he certainly came back again as wise as he went.

Well, Gentlemen, and what if we are called High-flyers now, and an Hundred Names of Contempt and Distinction, what is this to the purpose? who would not be a High-flyer, to be Tackt and Consolidated in an Engine of such sublime Elevation, and which lifts Men, Monarchs, Members, yea, and whole Nations, up into the Clouds; and performs with such wondrous Art, the long expected Experiment of a Voyage to the Moon? And thus much for the Description of the Consolidator.

The first Voyage I ever made to this Country, was in one of these Engines; and I can safely affirm, I never wak'd all the way; and now having been as often there as most that have us'd that Trade, it may be expected I should give some Account of the Country; for it appears, I can give but little of the Road.

Only this I understand, That when this Engine, by help of these Artificial Wings, has raised it self up to a certain height, the Wings are as useful to keep it from falling into the Moon, as they were before to raise it, and keep it from falling back into this Region again.

This may happen from an Alteration of Centers, and Gravity having past a certain Line, the Equipoise changes its Tendency, the Magnetick Quality being beyond it, it inclines of Course, and pursues a Center, which it finds in the Lunar World, and lands us safe upon the Surface.

I was told , I need take no Bills of Exchange with me,

nor Letters of Credit; for that upon my first Arrival, the Inhabitants would be very civil to me: That they never suffered any of Our World to want any thing when they came there: That they were very free to show them any thing, and inform them in all needful Cases; and that whatever Rarities the Country afforded, should be expos'd immediately.

I shall not enter into the Customs, Geography, or History of the Place, only acquaint the Reader, That I found no manner of Difference in any thing Natural, except as hereafter excepted, but all was exactly as is here, an Elementary World, peopled with Folks, as like us as if they were only Inhabitants of the same Continent, but in a remote Climate.

The Inhabitants were Men, Women, Beasts, Birds, Fishes, and Insects, of the same individual Species as Ours, the latter excepted: The Men no wiser, better, nor bigger than here; the Women no handsomer or honester than Ours: There were Knaves and honest Men, honest Women and Whores of all Sorts, Countries, Nations and Kindreds, as on this side the Skies.

They had the same Sun to shine, the Planets were equally visible as to us, and their Astrologers were as busily Impertinent as Ours, only that those wonderful Glasses hinted before made strange Discoveries that we were unacquainted with; by them they could plainly discover, That this World was their Moon, and their World our Moon; and when I came first among them, the People that flockt about me, distinguisht me by the Name of, the Man that came out of the Moon.

I cannot, however, but acquaint the Reader, with some

Remarks I made in this new World, before I come to any thing Historical.

I have heard, that among the Generallity of our People, who being not much addicted to Revelation, have much concern'd themselves about Demonstrations, a Generation have risen up, who to solve the Difficulties of Supernatural Systems, imagine a mighty vast Something, who has no Form but what represents him to them as one Great Eye: This infinite Optick they imagine to be Natura Naturans, or Power-forming; and that as we pretend the Soul of Man has a Similitude in quality to its Original, according to a Notion some People have, who read that so much ridicul'd Old Legend, call'd Bible, That Man was made in the Image of his Maker: The Soul of Man, therefore, in the Opinion of these Naturallists, is one vast Optick Power diffus'd through him into all his Parts, but seated principally in his Head.

From hence they resolve all Beings to Eyes, some more capable of Sight and receptive of Objects than others; and as to things Invisible, they reckon nothing so, only so far as our Sight is deficient, contracted or darkened by Accidents from without, as Distance of Place, Interposition of Vapours, Clouds, liquid Air, Exhalations, &c. or from within, as wandring Errors, wild Notions, cloudy Understandings, and empty Fancies, with a Thousand other interposing Obstacles to the Sight, which darken it, and prevent its Operation; and particularly obstruct the perceptive Faculties, weaken the Head, and bring Mankind in General to stand in need of the Spectacles of Education as soon as ever they are born: Nay, and as soon as they have made use of these Artificial Eyes, all they can do is but to clear the Sight so far as to see that they can't see; the utmost Wisdom of Mankind, and the highest Improvement a Man ought to wish for, being but to be able to see that he was Born blind; this pushes him upon search after Mediums for the Recovery of his Sight, and away he runs to School to Art and Science, and there he is furnisht with Horoscopes, Microscopes, Tellescopes, Caliscopes, Money-scopes, and the D - l and and all of Glasses, to help and assist his Moon-blind Understanding; these with wonderful Skill and Ages of Application, after wandring thro' Bogs and Wildernesses of Guess, Conjectures, Supposes, Calculations, and he knows not what, which he meets with in Physicks, Politicks, Ethicks, Astronomy, Mathematicks, and such sort of bewildring Things, bring him with vast Difficulty to a little Minute-spot, call'd Demonstration; and as not one in Ten Thousand ever finds the way thither, but are lost in the tiresome uncouth Journey, so they that do, 'tis so long before they come there, that they are grown Old and good for little in the Journey; and no sooner have they obtained a glimering of this Universal Eye-sight, this Eclaricissment General, but they Die, and have hardly time to show the way to those that come after.

Now, as the earnest search after this thing call'd Demonstration fill'd me with Desires of seeing every thing, so my Observations of the strange multitude of Mysteries I met with in all Men's Actions here, spurr'd my Curiosity to examine, if the Great Eye of the World had no People to whom he had given a clearer Eye-sight, or at least, that made a better use of it than we had here.

If pursuing this search I was much delighted at my Arrival into China, it cannot be thought strange, since there we find Knowledge as much advanc'd beyond our common Pitch, as it was pretended to be deriv'd from a more Ancient Original.

We are told, that in the early Age of the World, the Strength of Invention exceeded all that ever has been arrived to since: That we in these latter Ages, having lost all that pristine Strength of Reason and Invention, which died with the Ancients in the Flood, and receiving no helps from that Age, have by long Search arriv'd at several remote Parts of Knowledge, by the helps of reading Conversation and Experience; but that all amounts to no more than faint Imitations, Apings, and Resemblances of what was known in those masterly Ages.

Now, if it be true as is hinted before, That the Chinese Empire was Peopled long before the Flood; and that they were not destroyed in the General Deluge in the Days of Noah; 'tis no such strange thing, that they should so much out-do us in this sort of Eye-sight we call General Knowledge, since the Perfections bestow'd on Nature, when in her Youth and Prime met with no General Suffocation by that Calamity.

But if I was extreamly delighted with the extraordinary things I saw in those Countries, you cannot but imagine I was exceedingly mov'd, when I heard of a Lunar World; and that the way was passable from these Parts.

I had heard of a World in the Moon among some of our Learned Philosophers, and Moor, as I have been told, had a Moon in his Head; but none of the fine Pretenders, no not Bishop Wilkins, ever found Mechanick Engines, whose Motion was sufficient to attempt the Passage. A late happy Author indeed, among his Mechanick Operations of the Spirit, had found out an Enthusiasm, which if he could have pursued to its proper Extream, without doubt might, either in the Body or out of the Body, have Landed him somewhere hereabout; but that he form'd his System wholly upon the mistaken Notion of Wind, which Learned Hypothesis being directly contrary to the Nature of things in this Climate, where the Elasticity of the Air is quite different and where the pressure of the Atmosphere has for want of Vapour no Force, all his Notion dissolv'd in its Native Vapour call'd Wind, and flew upward in blew Strakes of a livid Flame call'd Blasphemy, which burnt up all the Wit and Fancy of the Author, and left a strange stench behind it, that has this unhappy quality in it, that every Body that Reads the Book, smells the Author, tho' he be never so far off; nay, tho' he took Shipping to Dublin, to secure his Friends from the least danger of a Conjecture.

But to return, to the happy Regions of the Lunar Continent, I was no sooner Landed there, and had lookt about me, but I was surpriz'd with the strange Alteration of the Climate and Country; and particularly a strange Salubrity and Fragrancy in the Air, which I felt so Nourishing, so Pleasant and Delightful, that tho' I could perceive some small Respiration, it was hardly discernable, and the least requisite for Life, supplied so long that the Bellows of Nature were hardly imployed.

But as I shall take occasion to consider this in a Critical Examination into the Nature, Uses and Advantages of Good Lungs, of which by it self, so I think fit to confine my present Observations to things more particularly concerning the Eye-sight.

I was, you may be sure, not a little surprized, when being upon an Eminence I found my self capable by common Observation, to see and distinguish things at the distance of 100 Miles and more, and seeking some Information on this point, I was acquainted by the People, that there was a certain grave Philosopher hard by, that could give me a very good Account of things.

It is not worth while to tell you this Man's Lunar Name, of whether he had a Name, or no; 'tis plain, 'twas a Man in the Moon; but all the Conference I had with him was very strange: At my first coming to him, he askt me if I came from the World in the Moon? I told him, no: At which he began to be angry, told me I Ly'd, he knew whence I came as well as I did; for he saw me all the way. I told him, I came to the World in the Moon, and began to be as surly as he. It was a long time before we could agree about it, he would have it, that I came down from the Moon; and I, that I came up to the Moon: From this, we came to Explications, Demonstrations, Spheres, Globes, Regions, Atmospheres, and a Thousand odd Diagrams, to make the thing out to one another. I insisted on my part, as that my Experiment qualified me to know, and challeng'd him to go back with me to prove it. He, like a true Philosopher, raised a Thousand Scruples, Conjectures, and Spherical Problems, to Confront me; and as for Demonstrations, he call'd 'em Fancies of my own. Thus we differ'd a great many ways; both of us were certain, and both uncertain; both right, and yet both directly contrary; how to reconcile this Jangle was very hard, till at last this Demonstration happen'd, the Moon as he call'd it, turning her blind-side upon us three Days after the Change, by which, with the help of his extraordinary Glasses, I that knew the Country, perceived that side the Sun lookt upon was all Moon, and the other was all world; and either I fancy'd I saw or else really saw all the lofty Towers of the Immense Cities of China: Upon this, and a little more Debate, we came to this Conclusion, and there the Old Man and I agreed, That they were both Moons and both Worlds, this a Moon to that, and that a Moon to this, like the Sun between two Looking-Glasses, and shone upon one another by Reflection, according to the oblique or direct Position of each other.

This afforded us a great deal of Pleasure; for all the World covet to be found in the right, and are pleas'd when their Notions are acknowledg'd by their Antagonists: It also afforded us many very useful Speculations, such as these;

1. How easy it is for Men to fall out, and yet all sides to be in the right?

2. How Natural it is for Opinion to despise Demonstration?

3. How proper mutual Enquiry is to mutual Satisfaction?

From the Observation of these Glasses, we also drew some Puns, Crotchets and Conclusions.

1st, That the whole World has a Blind-side, a Dark-side, and a Bright-side, and consequently so has every Body in it.

2dly, That the Dark-side of Affairs to Day, may be the Bright-side to Morrow; from whence abundance of useful Morals were also raised; such as,

1. No Man's Fate is so dark, but when the Sun shines upon it, it will return its Rays, and shine for it self.

2. All things turn like the Moon, up to Day, down to Morrow, Full and Change, Flux and Reflux.

3. Humane Understanding is like the Moon at the First Quarter, half dark.

3dly, The Changing-sides ought not to be thought so strange, or so much Condemn'd by Mankind, having its Original from the Lunar Influence, and govern'd by the Powerful Operation of Heavenly Motion.

4thly, If there be any such thing as Destiny in the World, I know nothing Man is so predestinated to, as to be eternally turning round; and but that I purpose to entertain the Reader with at least a whole Chapter or Section of the Philosophy of Humane Motion, Spherically and Hypocritically Examin'd and Calculated, I should inlarge upon that Thought in this place.

Having thus jumpt in our Opinions, and perfectly satisfied our selves with Demonstration, That these Worlds were Sisters, both in Form, Function, and all their Capacities; in short, a pair of Moons, and a pair of Worlds, equally Magnetical, Sympathetical, and Influential, we set up our rest as to that Affair, and went forward.

I desir'd no better Acquaintance in my new Travels, than this new Sociate; never was there such a Couple of People met; he was the Man in the Moon to me, and I the Man in the Moon to him; he wrote down all I said, and made a Book of it, and call'd it, News from the World in the Moon; and all the Town is like to see my Minutes under the same Title; nay, and I have been told, he published some such bold Truths there, from the Allegorical Relations he had of me from our World: That he was call'd before the Publick Authority, who could not bear the just Reflections of his damn'd Satyrical way of Writing; and there they punisht the Poor Man, put him in Prison, ruin'd his Family; and not only Fin'd him Ultra tenementum, but expos'd him in the high Places of their Capital City, for the Mob to laugh at him for a Fool: This is a Punishment not unlike our Pillory, and was appointed for mean Criminals, Fellows that Cheat and Couzen People, Forge Writings, Forswear themselves, and the like; and the People, that it was expected would have treated this Man very ill, on the contrary Pitied him, wisht those that set him there placed in his room, and exprest their Affections, by loud Shouts and Acclamations, when he was taken down.

But as this happen'd before my first Visit to that World, when I came there all was over with him, his particular Enemies were disgrac'd and turn'd out, and the Man was not at all the worse receiv'd by his Country-folks than he was before; and so much for the Man in the Moon.

After we had settled the Debate between us, about the Nature and Quality, I desir'd him to show me some Plan or Draft of this new World of his; upon which, he brought me out a pair of very beautiful Globes, and there I had an immediate Geographical Description of the Place.

I found it less by Degrees than Our Terrestial Globe, but more Land and less Water; and as I was particularly concern'd to see something in or near the same Climate with Our selves, I observ'd a large extended Country to the North, about the Latitude of 50 to 56 Northern Distance; and enquiring of that Country, he told me it was one of the best Countries in all their World: That it was his Native Climate, and he was just a going to it, and would take me with him.

He told me in General, the Country was Good, Wholsome, Fruitful, rarely Scituate for Trade, extraordinarily Accommodated with Harbours, Rivers and Bays for Shipping; full of Inhabitants; for it had been Peopled from all Parts, and had in it some of the Blood of all the Nations in the Moon.

He told me, as the Inhabitants were the most Numerous, so they were the strangest People that liv'd; both their Natures, Tempers, Qualities, Actions, and way of Living, was made up of innumerable Contradictions: That they were the Wisest Fools, and the Foolishest Wise Men in the World; the Weakest Strongest, Richest Poorest, most Generous Covetous, Bold Cowardly, False Faithful, Sober Dissolute, Surly Civil, Slothful Diligent, Peaceable Quarrelling, Loyal Seditious Nation that ever was known.

Besides my Observations which I made my self, and which could only furnish me with what was present, and which I shall take time to inform my Reader with as much Care and Conciseness as possible; I was beholding to this Old Lunarian, for every thing that was Historical or Particular.

And First, He inform'd me, That in this new Country they had very seldom any Clouds at all, and consequently no extraordinary Storms, but a constant

Serenity, moderate Breezes cooled the Air, and constant Evening Exhalations kept the Earth moist and fruitful; and as the Winds they had were various and strong enough to assist their Navigation, so they were without the Terrors, Dangers, Ship-wrecks and Destructions, which he knew we were troubled with in this our Lunar World, as he call'd it.

The first just Observation I made of this was, That I suppos'd from hence the wonderful Clearness of the Air, and the Advantage of so vast Optick Capacities they enjoy'd, was obtained: Alas! says the Old Fellow, You see nothing to what some of our Great Eyes see in some Parts of this World, nor do you see any thing compar'd to what you may see by the help of some new Invented Glasses, of which I may in time let you see the Experiment; and perhaps you may find this to be the reason why we do not so abound in Books as in your Lunar World; and that except it be some extraordinary Translations out of your Country, you will find but little in our Libraries, worth giving you a great deal of Trouble.

We immediately quitted the Philosophical Discourse of Winds, and I began to be mighty Inquisitive after these Glasses and Translations, and

1st, I understood here was a strange sort of Glass that did not so much bring to the Eye, as by I know not what wonderful Operation carried out the Eye to the Object, and quite varies from all our Doctrine of Opticks, by forming several strange Phanomena in Sight, which we are utterly unacquainted with; nor could Vision, Rarification, or any of our School-mens fine Terms, stand me in any stead in this case; but here was such Additions of piercing Organs, Particles of

Transparence, Emission, Transmission, Mediums, Contraction of Rays, and a Thousand Applications of things prepar'd for the wondrous Operation, that you may be sure are requisite for the bringing to pass something yet unheard of on this side the Moon.

First we were inform'd, by the help of these Glasses, strange things, which pass in our World for Non-Entities, is to be seen, and very perceptible; for Example:

State Polity, in all its Meanders, Shifts, Turns, Tricks, and Contraries, are so exactly Delineated and Describ'd, That they are in hopes in time to draw a pair of Globes out, to bring all those things to a certainty.

Not but that it made some Puzzle, even among these Clear-sighted Nations, to determine what Figure the Plans and Drafts of this undiscover'd World of Mysteries ought to be describ'd in: Some were of Opinion, it ought, to be an Irregular Centagon, a Figure with an Hundred Cones or Angles: Since the Unaccountables of this State-Science, are hid in a Million of undiscover'd Corners; as the Craft, Subtilty and Hypocrisy of Knaves and Courtiers have concealed them, never to be found out, but by this wonderful D - l-scope, which seem'd to threaten a perfect Discovery of all those Nudities, which have lain hid in the Embrio, and false Conceptions of Abortive Policy, ever since the Foundation of the World.

Some were of Opinion, this Plan ought to be Circular, and in a Globular Form, since it was on all sides alike, full of dark Spots, untrod Mazes, waking Mischiefs, and sleeping Mysteries; and being delineated like the

Globes display'd, would discover all the Lines of Wickedness to the Eye at one view: Besides, they fancied some sort of Analogy in the Rotundity of the Figure, with the continued Circular Motion of all Court-Policies, in the stated Round of Universal Knavery.

Others would have had it Hyrogliphical as by a Hand in Hand, the Form representing the Affinity between State Policy here, and State Policy in the Infernal Regions, with some unkind Similies between the Oeconomy of Satan's Kingdom, and those of most of the Temporal Powers on Earth; but this was thought too unkind. At last it was determin'd, That neither of these Schemes were capable of the vast Description; and that, therefore, the Drafts must be made single, tho' not dividing the Governments, yet dividing the Arts of Governing into proper distinct Schemes, viz.

1. A particular Plan of Publick Faith; and here we had the Experiment immediately made: The Representation is quallified for the Meridian of any Country, as well in our World as theirs; and turning it to'ards our own World, there I saw plainly an Exchequer shut up, and 20000 Mourning Families selling their Coaches, Horses, Whores, Equipages, &c. for Bread, the Government standing by laughing, and looking on: Hard by I saw the Chamber of a great City shut up, and Forty Thousand Orphans turn'd adrift in the World; some had no Cloaths, some no Shoes, some no Money; and still the City Magistrates calling upon other Orphans, to pay their money in. These things put me in mind of the Prophet Ezekiel, and methoughts I heard the same Voice that spoke to him, calling me, and telling me, Come hither, and I'll show thee greater Abominations than these: So looking still on that vast

Map, by the help of these Magnifying Glasses, I saw huge Fleets hir'd for Transport-Service, but never paid; vast Taxes Anticipated, that were never Collected; others Collected and Appropriated, but Misapplied: Millions of Talleys struck to be Discounted, and the Poor paying 40 per Cent, to receive their Money. I saw huge Quantities of Money drawn in, and little or none issued out; vast Prizes taken from the Enemy, and then taken away again at home by Friends; Ships sav'd on the Sea, and sunk in the Prize Offices; Merchants escaping from Enemies at Sea, and be Pirated by Sham Embargoes, Counterfeit Claims, Confiscations, &c a-shoar: There we saw Turkey-Fleets taken into Convoys, and Guarded to the very Mouth of the Enemy, and then abandon'd for their better Security: Here we saw Mons. Pouchartrain shutting up the Town-house of Paris, and plundring the Bank of Lyons.

2. Here we law the State of the War among Nations; Here was the French giving Sham-thanks for Victories they never got, and some body else adressing and congratulating the sublime Glory of running away: Here was Te Deum for Sham-Victories by Land; and there was Thanksgiving for Ditto by Sea: Here we might see two Armies fight, both run away, and both come and thank GOD for nothing: Here we saw a Plan of a late War like that in Ireland; there was all the Officers cursing a Dutch General, because the damn'd Rogue would fight, and spoil a good War, that with decent Management and good Husbandry, might have been eek't out this Twenty Years; there was whole Armies hunting two Cows to one Irishman, and driving of black Cattle declar'd the Noble End of the the War: Here we saw a Country full of Stone Walls and strong Towns, where every Campaign, the Trade of War was

carried on by the Soldiers, with the same Intriguing as it was carried on in the Council Chambers; there was Millions of Contributions raised, and vast Sums Collected, but no Taxes lessen'd; whole Plate Fleets surpriz'd, but no Treasure found; vaft Sums lost by Enemies, and yet never found by Friends, Ships loaded with Volatile Silver, that came away full, and gat home empty; whole Voyages made to beat No body, and plunder Every body; two Millions robb'd from the honest Merchants, and not a Groat sav'd for the honest Subjects: There we saw Captains Lifting Men with the Governments Money, and letting them go again for their own; Ships fitted out at the Rates of Two Millions a Year, to fight but once in Three Years, and then run away for want of Powder and Shot.

There we saw Partition Treaties damned, and the whole given away, Confederations without Allies, Allies without Quota's, Princes without Armies, Armies without Men, and Men without Money, Crowns without Kings, Kings without Subjects, more Kings than Countries, and more Countries than were worth fighting for.

Here we could see the King of France upbraiding his Neighbours with dishonourably assisting his Rebels, though the Mischief was, they did it not neither; and in the same Breath, assisting the Hungarian Rebels against the Emperor; M. Ld N. refusing so dishonourable an Action, as to aid the Rebellious Camisars, but Leaguing with the Admirant de Castile, to Invade the Dominions of his Master to whom he swore Allegiance: Here we saw Protestants fight against Protestants, to help Papists, Papists against Papists to help Protestants, Protestants call in Turks, to keep Faith against Christians that break it: Here we could see Swedes fighting for Revenge, and call it Religion; Cardinals deposing their Catholick Prince, to introduce the Tyranny of a Lutheran and call it Liberty; Armies Electing Kings, and call it Free Choice; French conquering Savoy, to secure the Liberty of Italy.

3. The Map of State Policy contains abundance of Civil Transactions, no where to be discover'd but in this wonderful Country, and by this prodigious Invention: As first, it shows an Eminent Prelate running in every body's Debt to relieve the Poor, and bring to God Robbery for Burnt-Offering: It opens a Door to the Fate of Nations; and there we might see the Duke of S - y bought three times, and his subjects sold every time; Portugal bought twice, and neither time worth the Earnest; Spain bought once, but loth to go with the Bidder; Venice willing to be Bought, if there had been any Buyers; Bavaria Bought, and run away with the Money; the Emperor Bought and Sold, but Bilkt the Chapman; the French buying Kingdoms he can't keep, the Dutch keep Kingdoms they never Bought; and the English paying their Money without Purchase.

In Matters of Civil Concerns, here was to be seen Religion with no out-side, and much Out-side with no Religion, much Strife about Peace, and no Peace in the Design: Here was Plunder without Violence, Violence without Persecution, Conscience without Good Works, and Good Works without Charity; Parties cutting one anothers Throats for God's Sake, pulling down Churches de propoganda fide, and making Divisions by way of Association.

Here we have Peace and Union brought to pass The Shortest Way, Extirpation and Destruction prov'd to be the Road to Plenty and Pleasure: Here all the Wise Nations, a Learned Author would have Quoted, if he could have found them, are to be seen, who carry on Exclusive Laws to the general Safety and Satisfaction of their Subjects.

Occasional Bills may have here a particular Historical, Categorical Description: But of them by themselves.

Here you might have the Rise, Original, Lawfulness, Usefulness, and Necessity of Passive Obedience, as fairly represented as a System of Divinity, and as clearly demonstrated as by a Geographical Description; and which exceeds our mean Understanding here, 'tis by the wonderful Assistance of these Glasses, plainly discerned to be Coherent with Resistance, taking Arms, calling in Foreign Powers, and the like. - Here you have a plain Discovery of C. of E. Politicks, and a Map of Loyalty: Here 'tis as plainly demonstrated as the Nose in a Man's Face, provided he has one, that a Man may Abdicate, drive away, and Dethrone his Prince, and yet be absolutely and intirely free from, and innocent of the least Fracture, Breach, Incroachment, or Intrenchment, upon the Doctrine of Non-Resistance: Can shoot at his Prince without any Design to kill him, fight against him without raising Rebellion, and take up Arms, without leaving War against his Prince.

Here they can persecute Dissenters, without desiring they should Conform, conform to the Church they would overthrow; Pray for the Prince they dare not Name, and Name the Prince they do not pray for.

By the help of these Glasses strange Insights are made, into the vast mysterious dark World of State Policy;

but that which is yet more strange, and requires vast Volumes to descend to the Particulars of, and huge Diagrams, Spheres, Charts, and a Thousand nice things to display is, That in this vast Intelligent Discovery it is not only made plain, that those things are so, but all the vast Contradictions are made Rational, reconciled to Practice, and brought down to Demonstration.

German Clock-Work, the perpetual Motions, the Prim Mobilies of Our short-sighted World, are Trifles to these Nicer Disquisitions.

Here it would be plain and rational, why a Parliament-Man will spend 5000 l. to be Chosen, that cannot get a Groat Honestly by setting there: It would be easily made out to be rational, why he that rails most at a Court is soonest receiv'd into it: Here it would be very plain, how great Estates are got in little Places, and Double in none at all. 'Tis easy to be prov'd honest and faithful to Victual the French Fleet out of English Stores, and let our own Navy want them; a long Sight, or a large Lunar Perspective, will make all these things not only plain in Fact, but Rational and Justifiable to all the World.

'Tis a strange thing to any body without doubt, that has not been in that clear-sighted Region, to comprehend, That those we call High-flyers in England are the only Friends to the Dissenters, and have been the most Diligent and Faithful in their Interest, of any People in the Nation; and yet so it is, Gentlemen, and they ought to have the Thanks of the whole Body for it.

In this advanc'd Station, we see it plainly by Reflexion, That the Dissenters, like a parcel of Knaves, have retained all the High-Church-men in their Pay; they are certainly all in their Pension-Roll: Indeed, I could not see the Money paid them there, it was too remote; but I could plainly see the thing; all the deep Lines of the Project are laid as true, they are so Tackt and Consolidated together, that if any one will give themselves leave to consider, they will be most effectually convinced, That the High-Church and the Dissenters here, are all in a Caball, a meer Knot, a piece of Clock-work; the Dissenters are the Dial-Plate, and the High-Church the Movement, the Wheel within the Wheels, the Spring and the Screw to bring all things to Motion, and make the Hand on the Dial-plate point which way the Dissenters please.

For what else have been all the Shams they have put upon the Governments, Kings, States, and People they have been concern'd with? What Schemes have they laid on purpose to be broken? What vast Contrivances, on purpose to be ridicul'd and expos'd? The Men are not Fools, they had never V - d to Consolidate a B - but that they were willing to save the Dissenters, and put it into a posture, in which they were sure it would miscarry. I defy all the Wise Men of the Moon to show another good reason for it.

Methinks I begin to pity my Brethren, the moderate Men of the Church, that they cannot see into this New Plot, and to wish they would but get up into our Consolidator, and take a Journey to the Moon, and there, by the help of these Glasses, they would see the Allegorical, Symbollical, Hetrodoxicallity of all this Matter; it would make immediate Converts of them; they would see plainly, that to Tack and Consolidate, to make Exclusive Laws, to persecute for Conscience, disturb, and distress Parties; these are all Phanatick Plots, meer Combinations against the Church, to bring her into Contempt, and to fix and establish the Dissenters to the end of the Chapter: But of this I shall find occasion to speak Occasionally, when an Occasion presents it self, to examine a certain Occasional Bill, transacting in these Lunar Regions, some time before I had the Happiness to arrive there.

In examining the Multitude and Variety of these most admirable Glasses for the assisting the Opticks, or indeed the Formation of a new perceptive Faculty; it was you may be sure most surprizing to find there, that Art had exceeded Nature; and the Power of Vision was assisted to that prodigious Degree, as even to distinguish Non-Entity it self; and in these strange Engines of Light it could not but be very pleasing, to distinguish plainly betwixt Being and Matter, and to come to a Determination, in the so long Canvast Dispute of Substance, vel Materialis, vel Spiritualis; and I can solidly affirm, That in all our Contention between Entity and Non-Entity, there is so little worth meddling with, that had we had these Glasses some Ages ago , we should have left troubling our heads with it.

I take upon me, therefore, to assure my Reader, That whoever pleases to take a Journey, or Voyage, or Flight up to these Lunar Regions, as soon as ever he comes ashoar there, will presently be convinc'd, of the Reasonableness of Immaterial Substance, and the Immortality, as well as Immateriality of the Soul: He will no sooner look into these Explicating Glasses, but he will be-able to know the separate meaning of Body, Soul, Spirit, Life, Motion, Death, and a Thousand things that Wise-men puzzle themselves about here, because they are not Fools enough to understand.

Here too I find Glasses for the Second Sight, as our Old Women call it. This Second Sight has been often pretended to in Our Regions, and some Famous Old Wives have told us, they can see Death, the Soul, Futurity, and the Neighbourhood of them, in the Countenance: By this wonderful Art, these good People unfold strange Mysteries, as under some Irrecoverable Disease, to foretell Death; under Hypocondriack Melancholy, to presage Trouble of Mind; in pining Youth, to predict Contagious Love; and an Hundred other Infallibilities, which never fail to be true as soon as ever they come to pass, and are all grounded upon the same Infallibility, by which a Shepherd may always know when any one of his Sheep is Rotten, viz. when he shakes himself to pieces.

But all this Guess and Uncertainty is a Trifle, to the vast Discoveries of these Explicatory Optick-Glasses; for here are seen the Nature and Consequences of Secret Mysteries: Here are read strange Mysteries relating to Predestination, Eternal Decrees, and the like: Here 'tis plainly prov'd, That Predestination is, in spight of all Enthusiastick Pretences, so intirely committed into Man's Power, that whoever pleases to hang himself to Day, won't Live till to Morrow: no, though Forty Predestination Prophets were to tell him, His time was not yet come. There abstruse Points are commonly and solemnly Discuss'd here; and these People are such Hereticks, that they say God's Decrees are all subservient to the means of his Providence; That what we call Providence is a subjecting all things to the great Chain of Causes and Consequences, by which that one Grand Decree, That all Effects shall Obey, without reserve to their proper moving Causes, supercedes all subsequent Doctrines, or pretended Decrees, or Predestination in the World: That by this

Rule, he that will kill himself, GOD, Nature, Providence, or Decree, will not be concern'd to hinder him, but he shall Die; any Decrees, Predestination, or Fore-Knowledge of Infinite Power, to the contrary in any wise, notwithstanding that it is in a Man's Power to throw himself into the Water, and be Drown'd; and to kill another Man, and he shall Die, and to say, God appointed it, is to make him the Author of Murther, and to injure the Murtherer in putting him to Death for what he could not help doing.

All these things are received Truths here, and no doubt would be so every where else, if the Eyes of Reason were opened to the Testimony of Nature, or if they had the helps of these most Incomparable Glasses.

Some pretended, by the help of these Second-sight Glasses, to see the common Periods of Life; and Others said, they could see a great way beyond the leap in the Dark: I confess, all I could see of the first was, that holding up the Glass against the Sea, I plainly saw, as it were on the edge of the Horizon, these Words,

> The Verge of Life and Death is here.
> 'Tis best to know where 'tis, but not how far.

As to seeing beyond Death, all the Glasses I lookt into for that purpose, made but little of it; and these were the only Tubes that I found Defective; for here I could discern nothing but Clouds, Mists, and thick dark hazy Weather; but revolving in my Mind, that I had read a certain Book in our own Country, called, Nature; it presently occurr'd, That the Conclusion of it, to all such as gave themselves the trouble of making out those foolish things call'd Inferences, was always Look up; upon which, turning one of their Glasses Up, and erecting the Point of it towards the Zenith, I saw these Words in the Air, REVELATION, in large Capital Letters.

I had like to have rais'd the Mob upon me for looking upright with this Glass; for this, they said, was prying into the Mysteries of the Great Eye of the World; That we ought to enquire no farther than he has inform'd us, and to believe what he had left us more Obscure: Upon this, I laid down the Glasses, and concluded, that we had Moses and the Prophets, and should be never the likelier to be taught by One come from the Moon.

In short, I found, indeed, they had a great deal more Knowledge of things than we in this World; and that Nature, Science, and Reason, had obtained great Improvements in the Lunar World; but as to Religion, it was the same equally resign'd to and concluded in Faith and Redemption; so I shall give the World no great Information of these things.

I come next to some other strange Acquirements obtained by the helps of these Glasses; and particularly for the discerning the Imperceptibles of Nature; such as, the Soul, Thought, Honesty, Religion, Virginity, and an Hundred other nice things, too small for humane Discerning.

The Discoveries made by these Glasses, as to the Soul, are of a very diverting Variety; some Hieroglyphical, and Emblematical, and some Demonstrative.

The Hieroglyphical Discoveries of the Soul make it appear in the Image of its Maker; and the Analogy is remarkable, even in the very Simily; for as they represent the Original of Nature as One Great Eye, illuminating as well as discerning all things; so the Soul, in its Allegorical, or Hieroglyphical Resemblance, appears as a Great Eye, embracing the Man, enveloping, operating, and informing every Part; from whence those sort of People who we falsly call Politicians, acting so much to put out this Great Eye, by acting against their common Understandings, are very aptly represented by a great Eye, with Six or Seven pair of Spectacles on; not but that the Eye of their Souls may be clear enough of it self, as to the common Understanding; but that they happen to have occasion to look sometimes so many ways at once, and to judge, conclude, and understand so many contrary ways upon one and the same thing; that they are fain to put double Glasses upon their Understanding, as we look at the Solar Ecclipses, to represent 'em in different Lights, least their Judgments should not be wheadled into a Compliance with the Hellish Resolutions of their Wills; and this is what I call the Emblematick Representation of the Soul.

As for the Demonstrations of the Soul's Existence, 'tis a plain case, by these Explicative Glasses, that it is, some have pretended to give us the Parts; and we have heard of Chyrurgeons, that could read an Anatomical Lecture on the Parts Of the Soul; and these pretend it to be a Creature in form, whether Camelion or Salamandar, Authors have not determin'd; nor is it compleatly discover'd when it comes into the Body, or how it goes out, or where its Locality or Habitation is, while 'tis a Resident.

But they very aptly show it, like a Prince, in his Seat, in the middle of his Palace the Brain, issuing out his incessant Orders to innumerable Troops of Nerves, Sinews, Muscles, Tendons, Veins, Arteries, Fibres,

Capilaris, and useful Officers, call'd Organici, who faithfully execute all the Parts of Sensation, Locomotion, Concoction, &c. and in the Hundred Thousandth part of a Moment, return with particular Messages for Information, and demand New Instructions. If any part of his Kingdom, the Body, suffers a Depredation, or an Invasion of the Enemy, the Expresses fly to the Seat of the Soul, the Brain, and immediately are order'd back to smart, that the Body may of course send more Messengers to complain; immediately other Expresses are dispatcht to the Tongue, with Orders to cry out, that the Neighbours may come in and help, or Friends send for the Chyrurgeon: Upon the Application, and a Cure, all is quiet, and the same Expresses are dispatcht to the Tongue to be hush, and say no more of it till farther Orders: All this is as plain to be seen in these Engines, as the Moon of Our World from the World in the Moon.

As the Being, Nature, and Scituation of humane Soul is thus Spherically and Mathematically discover'd, I could not find any Second Thoughts about it in all their Books, whether of their own Composition or by Translation; for it was a General received Notion, That there could not be a greater Absurdity in humane Knowledge, than to imploy the Thoughts in Questioning, what is as plainly known by its Consequences, as if seen with the Eye; and that to doubt the Being or Extent of the Soul's Operation, is to imploy her against her self; and therefore, when I began to argue with my Old Philosopher, against the Materiality and Immortality of this Mystery we call Soul, he laught at me, and told me, he found we had none of their Glasses in our World; and bid me send all our Scepticks, Soul-Sleepers, our Cowards, Bakers,

Kings and Bakewells, up to him into the Moon, if they wanted Demonstrations; where, by the help of their Engines, they would make it plain to them, that the Great Eye being one vast Intellect, Infinite and Eternal, all Inferior Life is a Degree of himself, and as exactly represents him as one little Flame the whole Mass of Fire; That it is therefore uncapable of Dissolution, being like its Original in Duration, as well as in its Powers and Faculties, but that it goes and returns by Emission, Regression, as the Great Eye governs and determines; and this was plainly made out, by the Figure I had seen it in, viz. an Eye, the exact Image of its Maker: 'Tis true, it was darkened by Ignorance, Folly and Crime, and therefore oblig'd to wear Spectacles; but tho' these were Defects or Interruptions in its Operation, they were none in its Nature; which as it had its immediate Efflux from the Great Eye, and its return to him must partake of himself, and could not but be of a Quality uncomatable, by Casualty or Death.

From this Discourse we the more willingly adjourned our present Thoughts, I being clearly convinced of the Matter; and as for our Learned Doctors, with their Second and Third Thoughts, I told him I would recommend them to the Man in the Moon for their farther Illumination, which if they refuse to accept, it was but just they should remain in a Wood, where they are, and are like to be, puzzling themselves about Demonstrations, squaring of Circles, and converting oblique into right Angles, to bring out a Mathematical Clock-Work Soul, that will go till the Weight is down, and then stand still till they know not who must wind it up again.

However, I cannot pass over a very strange and extraordinary piece of Art which this Old Gentleman inform'd me of, and that was an Engine to screw a Man into himself: Perhaps our Country-men may be at some Difficulty to comprehend these things by my dull Description; and to such I cannot but recommend, a Journey in my Engine to the Moon.

This Machine that I am speaking of, contains a multitude of strange Springs and Screws, and a Man that puts himself into it, is very insensibly carried into vast Speculations, Reflexions, and regular Debates with himself: They have a very hard Name for it in those Parts; but if I were to give it an English Name, it should be call'd, The Cogitator, or the Chair of Reflection.

And First, The Person that is seated here feels some pain in passing some Negative Springs, that are wound up, effectually to shut out all Injecting, Disturbing Thoughts; and the better to prepare him for the Operation that is to follow, and this is without doubt a very rational way; for when a Man can absolutely shut out all manner of thinking, but what he is upon, he shall think the more Intensly upon the one object before him.

This Operation past, here are certain Screws that draw direct Lines from every Angle of the Engine to the Brain of the Man, and at the same time, other direct Lines to his Eyes; at the other end of which Lines, there are Glasses which convey or reflect the Objects the Person is desirous to think upon.

Then the main Wheels are turn'd, which wind up according to their several Offices; this the Memory, that the Understanding; a third the Will, a fourth the thinking Faculty; and these being put all into regular

Motions, pointed by direct Lines to their proper Objects, and perfectly uninterrupted by the Intervention of Whimsy, Chimera, and a Thousand fluttering Damons that Gender in the Fancy, but are effectually Lockt out as before, assist one another to receive right Notions, and form just Ideas of the things they are directed to, and from thence the Man is impower'd to make right Conclusions, to think and act like himself, suitable to the sublime Qualities his Soul was originally blest with.

There never was a Man went into one of these thinking Engines, but he came wiser out than he was before; and I am persuaded, it would be a more effectual Cure to our Deism, Atheism, Scepticism, and all other Scisms, than ever the Italian's Engine, for Curing the Gout by cutting off the Toe.

This is a most wonderful Engine, and performs admirably, and my Author gave me extraordinary Accounts of the good Effects of it; and I cannot but tell my Reader, That our Sublunar World suffers Millions of Inconveniencies, for want of this thinking Engine: I have had a great many Projects in my Head, how to bring our People to regular thinking, but 'tis in vain without this Engin; and how to get the Model of it I know not; how to screw up the Will, the Understanding, and the rest of the Powers; how to bring the Eye, the Thought, the Fancy, and the Memory, into Mathematical Order, and obedient to Mechanick Operation; help Boyl, Norris, Newton, Manton, Hammond, Tillotson, and all the Learned Race, help Phylosophy, Divinity, Physicks, Oeconomicks, all's in vain, a Mechanick Chair of Reflection is the only Remedy that ever I found in my Life for this Work.

As to the Effects of Mathematical thinking, what Volumes might be writ of it will more easily appear, if we consider the wondrous Usefulness of this Engine in all humane Affairs; as of War, Peace, Justice, Injuries, Passion, Love, Marriage, Trade, Policy, and Religion.

When a Man has been screw'd into himself, and brought by this Art to a Regularity of Thought, he never commits any Absurdity after it; his Actions are squared by the same Lines, for Action is but the Consequence of Thinking; and he that acts before he thinks, sets humane Nature with the bottom upward.

M. would never have made his Speech, nor the famous B - ly wrote a Book, if ever they had been in this thinking Engine: One would have never told us of Nations he never saw, nor the other told us, he had seen a great many, and was never the Wiser.

H. had never ruin'd his Family to Marry Whore, Thief and Beggar-Woman, in one Salliant Lady, after having been told so honestly, and so often of it by the very Woman her self.

Our late unhappy Monarch had never trusted the English Clergy, when they preacht up that Non-Resistance, which he must needs see they could never Practice; had his Majesty been screw'd up into this Cogitator, he had presently reflected, that it was against Nature to expect they should stand still, and let him tread upon them: That they should, whatever they had preacht or pretended to, hold open their Throats to have them be cut , and tye their own Hands from resisting the Lord's Anointed.

Had some of our Clergy been screw'd in this Engine,

they had never turned Martyrs for their Allegiance to the Late King, only for the Lechery of having Dr. S - in their Company.

Had our Merchants been manag'd in this Engine, they had never trusted their Turkey Fleet with a famous Squadron, that took a great deal of care to Convoy them safe into the Enemies Hands.

Had some People been in this Engine, when they had made a certain League in the World, in order to make amends for a better made before, they would certainly have consider'd farther, before they had embarkt with a Nation, that are neither fit to go abroad nor stay at Home.

As for the Thinking practis'd in Noble Speeches, Occasional Bills, Addressings about Prerogative, Convocation Disputes, Turnings in and Turnings out at Ours, and all the Courts of Christendom, I have nothing to say to it.

Had the Duke of Bavaria been in our Engine, he would never have begun a Quarrel, which he knew all the Powers of Europe were concern'd to suppress, and lay all other Business down till it was done.

Had the Elector of Saxony past the Operation of this Engine, he would never have beggar'd a Rich Electorate, to ruin a beggar'd Crown, nor sold himself for a Kingdom hardly worth any Man's taking: He would never have made himself less than he was, in hopes of being really no greater; and stept down from a Protestant Duke, and Imperial Elector, to be a Nominal Mock King with a shadow of Power, and a Name without honour, Dignity or Strength.

Had Mons. Tallard been in our Engine, he would not only not have attackt the Confederates when they past the Morass and Rivulet in his Front, but not have attackt them at all, nor have suffer'd them to have attackt him, it being his Business not to have fought at all, but have linger'd out the War, till the Duke of Savoy having been reduced, the Confederate Army must have been forced to have divided themselves of course, in order to defend their own.

Some that have been very forward to have us proceed The Shortest Way with the Scots, may be said to stand in great need of this Chair of Reflection, to find out a just Cause for such a War, and to make a Neighbour-Nation making themselves secure, a sufficient Reason for another Neighbour-Nation to fall upon them: Our Engine would presently show it them in a clear sight, by way of Paralel, that 'tis just with the fame Right as a Man may break open a House, because the People bar and bolt the Windows.

If some-body has chang'd Hands there from bad to worse, and open'd instead of closing Differences in those Cases, the Cogitator migyt have brought them, by more regular Thinking, to have known that was not at all the Method of bringing the S - s to Reason.

Our Cogitator would be a very necessary thing to show some People, That Poverty and Weakness is not a sufficient Ground to oppress a Nation, and their having but little Trade, cannot be a sufficient Ground to equip Fleets to take away what they have.

I cannot deny, that I have often thought they have had something of this Engine in our Neighbouring Antient Kingdom, since no Man, however we pretend to be angry, but will own they are in the right of it, as to themselves, to Vote and procure Bills for their own Security, and not to do as others demand without Conditions fit to be accepted: But of that by it self.

There are abundance of People in Our World, of all sorts and Conditions, that stand in need of our thinking Engines, and to be screw'd into themselves a little, that they might think as directly as they speak absurdly: But of these also in a Class by it self.

This Engine has a great deal of Philosophy in it; and particularly, 'tis a wonderful Remedy against Poreing; and as it was said of Mons. Jurieu at Amsterdam, that he us'd to lose himself in himself; by the Assistance of this piece of Regularity, a Man is most effectually secur'd against bewildring Thoughts, and by direct thinking, he prevents all manner of dangerous wandring, since nothing can come to more speedy Conclusions, than that which in right Lines, points to the proper Subject of Debate.

All sorts of Confusion of Thoughts are perfectly avoided and prevented in this case, and a Man is never troubled with Spleen, Hyppo, or Mute Madness, when once he has been thus under the Operation of the Screw: It prevents abundance of Capital Disasters in Men, in private Affairs; it prevents hasty Marriages, rash Vows, Duels, Quarrels, Suits at Law, and most sorts of Repentance. In the State, it saves a Government from many Inconveniences; it checks immoderate Ambition, stops Wars, Navies and Expeditions; especially it prevents Members making long Speeches when they have nothing to say; it keeps back Rebellions, Insurrections, Clashings of Houses, Occasional Bills, Tacking, &c.

It has a wonderful Property in our Affairs at Sea, and has prevented many a Bloody Fight, in which a great many honest Men might have lost their Lives that are now useful Fellows, and help to Man and manage Her Majesty's Navy.

What if some People are apt to charge Cowardice upon some People in those Cases? 'Tis plain that cannot be it, for he that dare incur the Resentment of the English Mob, shows more Courage than would be able to carry him through Forty Sea-fights.

'Tis therefore for want of being in this Engine, that we censure People, because they don't be knocking one another on the Head, like the People at the Bear-Garden; where, if they do not see the Blood run about, they always cry out, A Cheat; and the poor Fellows are fain to cut one another, that they may not be pull'd a pieces; where the Case is plain, they are bold for fear, and pull up Courage enough to Fight, because they are afraid of the People.

This Engine prevents all sorts of Lunacies, Love-Frenzies, and Melancholy-Madness, for preserving the Thought in right Lines to direct Objects, it is impossible any Deliriums, Whimsies, or fluttering Air of Ideas, can interrupt the Man, he can never be Mad; for which reason I cannot but recommend it to my Lord S - , my Lord N - , and my Lord H - , as absolutely necesssary to defend them from the State-Madness, which for some Ages has possest their Families, and which runs too much in the Blood.

It is also an excellent Introduction to Thought, and therefore very well adapted to those People whose peculiar Talent and Praise is, That they never think at all. Of these, if his Grace of B - d would please to accept Advice from the Man in the Moon, it should be to put himself into this Engine, as a Soveraign Cure to the known Disease call'd the Thoughtless Evil.

But above all, it is an excellent Remedy, and very useful to a sort of People, who are always Travelling in Thought, but never Deliver'd into Action; who are so exceeding busy at Thinking, they have no leisure for Action; of whom the late Poet sung well to the purpose;

- Some modern Coxcombs, who
Retire to Think, 'cause they have nought to do;
For Thoughts were giv'n for Actions Government,
Where Action ceases, Thought Impertinent:
The Sphere of Action is Life's Happiness,
And he that Thinks beyond, Thinks like an Ass.
Rochest. Poems, p. 9.

These Gentlemen would make excellent use of this Engine, for it would teach 'em to dispatch one thing before they begin another; and therefore is of singular use to honest S - , whose peculiar it was, to be always beginning Projects, but never finish any.

The Variety of this Engine, its Uses, and Improvements, are Innumerable, and the Reader must not expect I can give any thing like a perfect Description of it.

There are yet another sort of Machine, which I never obtained a sight of, till the last Voyage I made to this Lunar Orb, and these are called Elevators: The Mechanick Operations of these are wonderful, and helpt by Fire; by which the Sences are raised to all the strange Extreames we can imagine, and whereby the Intelligent Soul is made to converse with its own Species, whether embody'd or not.

Those that are rais'd to a due pitch in this wondrous Frame, have a clear Prospect into the World of Spirits, and converse with Visions, Guardian-Angels, Spirits departed, and what not: And as this is a wonderful Knowledge, and not to be obtained, but by the help of this Fire; so those that have try'd the Experiment, give strange Accounts of Sympathy, Prexistence of Souls, Dreams, and the like.

I confess, I always believ'd a converse of Spirits, and have heard of some who have experienced so much of it, as they could obtain upon no Body else to believe.

I never saw any reason to doubt the Existent State of the Spirit before embody'd, any more than I did of its Immortality after it shall be uncas'd, and the Scriptures saying, the Spirit returns to God that gave it, implies a coming from, or how could it be call'd a return.

Nor can I see a reason why Embodying a Spirit should altogether Interrupt its Converse with the World of Spirits, from whence it was taken; and to what else shall we ascribe Guardian Angels, in which the Scripture is also plain; and from whence come Secret Notices, Impulse of Thought, pressing Urgencies of Inclination, to or from this or that altogether Involuntary; but from some waking kind Assistant wandring Spirit, which gives secret hints to its Fellow-Creature, of some approaching Evil or Good, which it was not able to foresee.

For Spirits without the helps of Voice converse.

I know we have supplied much of this with Enthusiasm and conceited Revelation; but the People of this World convince us, that it may be all Natural, by obtaining it in a Mechanick way, viz. by forming something suitable to the sublime Nature, which working by Art, shall only rectify the more vigorous Particles of the Soul, and work it up to a suitable Elevation. This Engine is wholly applied to the Head, and Works by Injection; the chief Influence being on what we call Fancy, or Imagination, which by the heat of strong Ideas, is fermented to a strange heighth, and is thus brought to see backward and forward every way, beyond it self: By this a Man fancies himself in the Moon, and realizes things there as distinctly, as if he was actually talking to my Old Phylosopher.

This indeed is an admirable Engine, 'tis compos'd of an Hundred Thousand rational Consequences, Five times the number of Conjectures, Supposes, and Probabilities, besides an innumerable Company of fluttering Suggestions, and Injections, which hover round the Imagination, and are all taken in as fast as they can be Concocted and Digested there: These are form'd into Ideas, and some of those so well put together, so exactly shap'd, so well drest and set out by the Additional Fire of Fancy, that it is no uncommon thing for the Person to be intirely deceived by himself, not knowing the brat of his own Begetting, nor be able to distinguish between Reality and Representation: From hence we have some People talking to Images of their own forming, and seeing more Devils and Spectres than ever appear'd: From hence we have weaker Heads not able to bear the Operation, seeing imperfect Visions, as of Horses and Men without Heads or Arms, Light without Fire, hearing Voices without Sound, and Noises without Shapes, as their own Fears or Fancies broke the Phanomena before the intire Formation.

But the more Genuine and perfect Use of these vast Elevations of the Fancy, which are perform'd, as I said, by the Mechanick Operation of Innate Fire, is to guide Mankind to as much Fore-sight of things, as either by Nature, or by the Aid of any thing Extranatural, may be obtain'd; and by this exceeding Knowledge, a Man shall forebode to himself approaching Evil or Good, so as to avoid this, or be in the way of that; and what if I should say, That the Notices of these things are not only frequent, but constant, and require nothing of us, but to make use of this Elevator, to keep our Eyes, our Ears, and our Fancies open to the hints; and observe them;

You may suppose me, if you please, come by this time into those Northern Kingdoms I mention'd before, where my Old Philosopher was a Native, and not to trouble you with any of the needful Observations, Learned Inscriptions, &c. on the way, according to the laudable practices of the Famous Mr. Br - mly, 'tis sufficient to tell you I found there an Opulent, Populous, Potent and Terrible People.

I found them at War with one of the greatest Monarchs of the Lunar World, and at the same time miserably rent and torn, mangl'd and disorder'd among themselves.

As soon as I observ'd the Political posture of their Affairs, (for here a Man sees things mighty soon by the helps of such a Masterly Eye-sight as I have mention'd) and remembring what is said for our Instruction, That a Kingdom divided against its self cannot stand; I ask'd the Old Gentleman if he had any

Estate in that Country? He told me, no great matter; but ask'd me why I put that Question to him? Because, said I, if this People go on fighting and snarling at all the World, and one among another in this manner, they will certainly be Ruin'd and Undone, either subdu'd by some more powerful Neighbour; whilst one Party will stand still and see the t'others Throat cut, tho' their own Turn immediately follows, or else they will destroy and devour one another. Therefore I told him I would have him Turn his Estate into Money, and go some where else; or go back to the other World with me.

No, no, reply'd the Old Man, I am in no such Fear at this Time, the Scale of Affairs is very lately chang'd here, says he, in but a very few Years.

I know nothing of that, said I, but I am sure there never was but one spot of Ground in that World which I came from, that was divided like them, and that's that very Country I liv'd in. Here are three Kingdoms of you in one spot, said I, One has already been Conquer'd and Subdu'd, the t'other suppres'd its Native lnhabitants, and planted it with her own, and now carries it with so high a Hand over them of her own Breed, that she limits their Trade, stops their Ports, when the Inhabitants have made their Manufactures, these wont give them leave to send them abroad, impose Laws upon them, refuse to alter and amend those they would make for themselves, make them pay Customs, Excises, and Taxes, and yet pay the Garrisons and Guards that defend them, themselves; Press their Inhabitants to their Fleets, and carry away their Old Veteran Troops that should defend them, and leave them to raise more to be serv'd in the same manner, will let none of their Mony be carry'd over thither, nor let them Coin any of their own; and a great many such hardships they suffer under the Hand of this Nation as meer Slaves and Conquer'd People, tho' the greatest part of the Traders are the People of the very Nation that treats 'em thus.

On the other hand, this creates Eternal Murmurs, Heart-burnings and Regret, both in the Natives and the Transplanted Inhabitants; the first have shewn their Uneasiness by frequent Insurrections and Rebellions, for Nature prompts the meanest Animal to struggle for Liberty; and these struggles have often been attended with great Cruelty, Ravages, Death, Massacres, and Ruin both of Families and the Country it self: As to the Transplanted Inhabitants, they run into Clandestine Trade, into corresponding with their Masters Enemies, Victualling their Navies, Colonies and the like, receiving and importing their Goods in spight of all the Orders and Directions to the contrary.

These are the effects of Divisions, and Feuds on that side; on the other hand there is a Kingdom Entire Unconquer'd and Independent, and for the present, under the same Monarch with the rest. - But here their Feuds are greater than with the other, and more dangerous by far because National: This Kingdom joins to the North part of the first Kingdom, and Terrible Divisions ly among the two Nations.

The People of these two Kingdoms are call'd if you please for distinction sake, for I cannot well make you understand their hard Names, Solunarians and Nolunarians, these to the South and those to the North, the Solunarians were divided in their Articles of Religion; the Governing Party, or the Establish'd Church, I shall call the Solunarian Church; but the whole Kingdom was full of a sort of Religious People call'd Crolians, who like our Dissenters in England profess divers sub-divided Opinions by themselves, and cou'd not, or wou'd not, let it go which way it will, joyn with the Establish'd Church.

On the other hand, the Establish'd Church in the Northern Kingdom was all Crolians, but full of Solunarians in Opinions, who were Dissenters there, as the Crolians were Dissenters in the South, and this unhappy mixture occasion'd endless Feuds, Divisions, Sub-divisions and Animosities without Number, of which hereafter.

The Northern Men are Bold, Terrible Numerous and Brave, to the last Degree, but Poor, and by the Encroachments of their Neighbours, growing poorer every Day.

The Southern are equally Brave, more Numerous and Terrible, but Wealthy and care not for Wars, had rather stay at Home and Quarrel with one another, than go Abroad to Fight, making good an Old Maxim, Too Poor t'Agree, and yet too Rich to Fight.

Between these the Feud is great, and every Day growing greater; and those People who pretend to have been in the Cogitator or thinking Engine tell us, all the lines of Consequences in that Affair point at a fatal period between the Kingdoms.

The Complaints also are great, and back'd with fiery Arguments on both sides; the Northern Men say, the Solunarians have dealt unjustly and unkindly by them in several Articles; but the Southern Men reply with a most powerful Argument, viz. they are Poor, and therefore ought to be Oppress'd , Suppress'd, or any thing.

But the main Debate is like to lye upon the Article of Choosing a King; both the Nations being under one Government at present, but the Settlement ending in the Reigning Line, the Northern Men refuse to joyn in Government again, unless they have a rectification of some Conditions in which, they say, they have the worst of it.

In this case, even the Southern Men themselves, say, they believe the Nolunarians have been in the Chair of Reflection, the thinking Engine, and that having screw'd their Understandings into a Direct Position to that Matter before them, they have made a right Judgment of their own Affairs, and with all their Poverty stand on the best Foot as to Right.

But as the matter of this Northern Quarrel comes under a Second Head, and is more properly the Subject of a Second Voyage to the Moon; the Reader may have it more at large consider'd in another Class, and some farther Enlightnings in that Affair than perhaps can be reasonably expected of me here.

But of all the Feuds and Brangles that ever poor Nation was embroild in, of all the Quarrels, the Factions and Parties that ever the People of any Nation thought worth while to fall out for, none were ever in reality so light, in effect so heavy, in appearance so great, in substance so small, in name so terrible, in nature so trifling, as those for which this Southern Country was altogether by the Ears among themselves.

And this was one Reason why I so earnestly enquir'd of my Lunarian Philosopher, whether he had an Estate in that Country or no. But having told him the Cause of that enquiry, he reply'd, there was one thing in the Nature of his Country-men which secur'd them from the ruin which usually attended divided Nations, viz. that if any Foreign Nation thinking to take the advantage of their Intestine Divisions fell upon them in the highest of all their Feuds, they'd lay aside their Parties and Quarrels and presently fall in together to beat out the common Enemy; and then no sooner had they obtain'd Peace abroad, by their Conduct and Bravery, but they would fall to cutting one anothers Throats again at home as naturally as if it had been their proper Calling, and that for Trifles too, meer Trifles.

Very well, said I to my learned Self, pretty like my own Country still, that whatever Peace they have abroad, are sure to have none at home.

To come at the historical Account of these Lunarian Dissentions, it will be absolutely necessary to enter a little into the Story of the Place, at least as far as relates to the present Constitution, both of the People, the Government, and the Subject of their present Quarrels.

And first we are to understand, that there has for some Ages been carry'd on in these Countries, a private feud or quarrel among the People, about a thing call'd by them Upogyla, with us very vulgarly call'd Religion.

This Difference, as in its Original it was not great, nor indeed upon Points accounted among themselves Essential, so it had never been a Difference of any height, if there had not always been some one thing, or other, hapning in the State which made the Court-Polititians think it necessary to keep the People busy and embroil'd, to prevent their more narrow Inspection into Depredations and Encroachments on their Liberties, which was always making on them by the Court.

'Tis not deny'd but there might be a Native want of Charity in the Inhabitant, adapting them to Feud, and particularly qualifying them to be alwavs Piquing one another; and some of their own Nation, who by the help of the famous Perspectives before-mentioned, pretend to have seen farther into the Insides of Nature and Constitution than other People, tell us the cross Lines of Nature which appear in the make of those particular People, signify a direct Negative as to the Article of Charity and good Neighbour-hood.

'Twas particularly unhappy to this wrangling People, that Reasons of State should always fall in, to make that uncharitableness and continual quarrelling Humour necessary to carry on the Publick Affairs of the Nation, and may pass for a certain Proof, that the State was under some Diseases and Convulsions, which, like a Body that digests nothing so well as what is hurtful to its Constitution, makes use of those things for its Support, which are in their very Nature, fatal to its being, and must at last tend to its Destruction.

But as this however enclin'd them to be continually Snarling at one another, so as in all Quarrels it generally appears one Side must go down.

The prevailing Party therefore always kept the Power in their Hands, and as the under were always Subject to the lash they soon took care to hook their Quarrel into the Affairs of State, and so join Religious Differences, and Civil Differences together.

These things had long embroil'd the Nation, and frequently involv'd them in bitter Enmities, Feuds, and Quarrels, and once in a tedious, ruinous, and bloody War in their own Bowels, in which, contrary to all expectation, this lesser Party prevail'd.

And since the allegorick Relation may bear great Similitude with our European Affairs on this side the Moon: I shall for the ease of Expression, and the better Understanding of the Reader, frequently call them by the same Names our unhappy Parties are call'd by in England, as Solunnarian Churchmen, and Crolian Dissenters, at the same time desiring my Reader to observe, that he is always to remember who it is we are talking of, and that he is by no means to understand me of any Person, Party, People, Nation, or Place on this side the Moon, any Expression, Circumstance, Similitude, or Appearance to the contrary in any wise notwithstanding.

This premis'd, I am to tell the Reader that the last Civil War in this Lunar Country ended in the Victors confounding their own Conquests by their intestine Broils, they being as is already noted a most Eternally Quarrelling Nation; upon this new Breach, they that first began the War, turn'd about, and pleading that they took up Arms to regulate the Government, not to overthrow it, fell in with the Family of their Kings, who had been banish'd, and one of them destroy'd, and restor'd the Crown to the Family, and the Nation to the Crown, just for all the World as the Presbyterians in England did, in the Case of King Charles the Second.

The Party that was thus restor'd, accepted the return the others made to their Duty, and their Assistance in restoring the Family of their Monarch, but abated not a

Tittle of the old Rancour against them as a Party which they entertain'd at their first taking Arms, not allowing the return they had made to be any attonement at all for the Crimes they had been guilty of before. 'Tis true they pass'd an Act or Grant of General Pardon, and Oblivion, as in all such Cases is usual, and as without which the other would never ha' come in, or have join'd Powers to form the Restoration they were bringing to pass, but the old Feud of Religion continu'd with this addition, that the Dissenters were Rebels, Murtherers, King-killers, Enemies to Monarchy and Civil Government, lovers of Confusion, popular, anarchial Governments, and movers of Sedition; that this was in their very Nature and Principles, and the like.

In this Condition, and under these Mortifications this Party of People liv'd just an Egyptian Servitude, viz. of 40 Years, in which time they were frequently vex'd with Persecution, Harass'd, Plunder'd, Fin'd, Imprisoned, and very hardly Treated, insomuch that they pretend to be able to give an account of vast Sums of their Country-Mony, levy'd upon them on these Occasions, amounting as I take it to 2 Millions of Lunatians, a Coin they keep their Accounts by there, and much about the value of our Pound Sterling; besides this they were hook't into a great many Sham Plots, and Sworn out of their Lives and Estates in such a manner, that in the very next Reign the Government was so sensible of their hard treatment, that they revers'd several Sentences by the same Authority that had Executed them; a most undeniable Proof they were asham'd of what had been done; at last, the Prince who was restor'd as abovesaid, dyed, and his Brother mounted the Throne; and now began a third Scene of Affairs, for this Prince was neither Church-man, nor

Dissenter, but of a different Religion from them all, known in that Country by the Name of Abrogratzianism, and this Religion of his had this one absolutely necessary Consequence in it, that a Man could not be sincerely and heartily of this, but he must be an Implacable hater of both the other. As this is laid down as a previous Supposition, we are with the same Reason to imagine this Prince to be entirely bent upon the Suppression and Destruction of both the other, if not absolutely as to Life and Estate, yet entirely as to Religion.

To bring this the more readily to pass like a true Polititian, had his Methods and Particulars been equally Politick with his Generals, he began at the right End, viz. to make the Breach between the Solunnarian Church, and the Crolian Dissenters as wide as possible, and to do this it was resolv'd to shift Sides, and as the Crown had always took part with the Church, crush'd, humbl'd, persecuted, and by all means possible mortify'd the Dissenters, as is noted in the Reign of his Predecessor. This Prince resolv'd to caress, cherish, and encourage the Crolians by all possible Arts and outward Endearments, not so much that they purpos'd them any real Favour, for the destruction of both was equally determin'd, nor so much that they expected to draw them over to Abrogratzianism, but Two Reasons may be suppos'd to give Rise to this Project.

1. The Lunarian Church Party had all along Preach'd up for a part of their Religion, that Absolute undisputed Obedience, was due from every Subject to their Prince without any Reserve, Reluctance or Repining; that as to Resistance, it was Fatal to Body, Soul, Religion, Justice and Government; and tho' the

Doctrine was Repugnant to Nature, and to the very Supreme Command it self, yet he that resisted, receiv'd to himself Damnation, just for all the World like our Doctrine of Passive Obedience. Now tho' these Solunarian Church-Men did not absolutely believe all they said themselves to be true, yet they found it necessary to push these things to the uttermost Extremities, because they might the better fix upon the Crolian Dissenters, the Charge of professing less Loyal Principles than they. For as to the Crolians, they profess'd openly they would pay Obedience to the Prince, as far as the Laws directed, but no farther.

These things were run up to strange heights, and the People were always falling out about what they would do, or wou'd not do, if things were so or so, as they were not, and were never likely to be; and the hot Men on both sides were every now and then going together by the Ears about Chimeras, Shadows, May-be's and Supposes.

The hot Men of the Solunarian Church were for knocking the Crolians in the Head, because as they said they were Rebels, their Fathers were Rebels, and they would certainly turn Rebels again upon occasion.

The Crolians insisted upon it, that they had nothing to do with what was done before they were Born, that if they were Criminal, because their Fathers were so, then a great many who were now of the Solunarian Church were as Guilty as they, several of the best Members of that Church having been Born of Crolian Parents.

In the matter of Loyalty they insisted upon it, they were as Loyal as the Solunarians, for that they were as

Loyal as Nature, Reason and the Laws both of God and Man requir'd, and what the Other talk'd of more, was but a meer pretence, and so it would be found if ever their Prince should have occasion to put them to the Tryal, that he that pretended to go beyond the Power of Nature and Reason, must indeed go beyond them, and they never desir'd to be brought into the extream, but they were ready at any time to shew such Proofs, and give such Demonstrations of their Loyalty, as would satisfy any reasonable Prince, and for more they had nothing to say.

In this posture of Affairs, this new Prince found his Subjects when he came to the Crown, the Solunarian Church Caress'd him, and notwithstanding his being Devoted to the Abrogratzian Faith, they Crown'd him with extraordinary Acclamations.

They were the rather enclin'd to push this forward by how much they thought it would singularly mortify the Crolians, and all the sorts of Dissenters, for they had all along declar'd their abhorrence of the Abrogratzians to such a Degree that they publickly endeavour'd to have got a general Concurrence of the whole Nation in the Publick Cortez, or Dyet of the Kingdom, to have joyn'd with them in Excluding this very Prince by Name, and all other Princes that should ever embrace the Abrogratzian Faith.

And it wanted but a very little of bringing it to pass, for almost all the Great Men of the Nation, tho' Solunarians, yet that were Men of Temper, Moderation, and Fore-sight, were for this exclusive Law. But the High Priests and Patriarchs of the Solunarian Church prevented it, and upon pretence of this Passive Obedience Principle, made their Interest and gave their Voices for Crowning, or Entailing the Crown and Government on the Head of one of the most Implacable Enemies both to their Religion and Civil Right that ever the Nation saw; but they liv'd to Repent it too late.

This Conquest over the Crolians and the Moderate Solunarians, if it did not suppress them entirely, it yet gave the other Part such an ascendant over them, that they made no Doubt when that Prince came to the Crown, they had done so much to oblige him, that he could deny them nothing, and therefore in expectation they swallow'd up the whole Body of the Crolians at once, and began to talk of nothing less than Banishing them to the Northern part of the Country, or to certain Islands, and Countries a vast way off, where formerly great numbers of them had fled for shelter in like Cases.

And this was the more probable by an unhappy Stroke these Crolians attempted to strike, but miscarry'd in at the very beginning of this Prince's Reign: for as they had always profest an aversion to this Prince on account of his Religion, as soon as their other King was dead, they set up one of his Natural Sons against this King, which the Solunarians had so joyfully Crown'd. This young Prince invaded his Dominions, and great Numbers of the most zealous Crolians joyn'd him - But to cut the Story short, he was entirely routed by the Forces of the new Prince, for all the Solunarian Church joyn'd with him against the Crolians without any respect to the Interest of Religion, so they overthrew their Brethren: The young invaded Prince was taken and put to Death openly, and Great Cruelties were exercis'd in cold Blood upon the poor unhappy People that were taken in the Defeat!

Thus a second time these Loyal Solunarian Churchmen Establish'd their Enemy, and built up what they were glad afterwards to pull down again, and to beg the assistance of those Crolians whom they had so rudely handled, to help them demolish the Power they had erected themselves, and which now began to set its foot upon the Throat of those that nourish'd and supported it.

Upon this exceeding Loyalty and blind Assistance given to their Prince, the Solunarians made no question but they had so Eternally bound him to them, that it would be in their Power to pull down the very Name of Crolianism, and utterly destroy it from the Nation.

But the time came on to Undeceive them, for this Prince, whose Principle as an Abrogratzian, was to destroy them both, as it happened, was furnish'd with Counsellors and Ecclesiasticks of his own Profession, ten thousand Times more bent for their general Ruin, than himself.

For abstracted from the Venom and Rancour of his Profession as an Abrogratzian, and from the furious Zeal of his Bramin, Priests, and Religious People, that continually hung about him, and that prompted him to act against his Temper and Inclination, by which he ruin'd all, he was else a forward and generous Prince, and likely to have made his People Great and Flourishing.

But his furious Church-Men ruin'd all his good Designs, and turn'd all his Projects to compass the Introduction of his own Religion into his Dominions.

Nay, and had he not fatally been push'd on by such as

really design'd his Ruin, to drive this deep Design on too hastily and turn the Scale of his Management from a close and conceal'd, to an open and profess'd Design, he might have gone a great way with it. Had he been content to have let that have been twenty Year a doing, which he impatiently as well as preposterously attempted all at once. Wise Men have thought he might in time have supprest the Solunarian Religion, and have set up his own.

To give a short Scheme of his Proceedings, and with them of the reason of his Miscarriage.

1. Having defeated the Rebellious Crolians, as is before noted, and reflecting on the Danger he was in upon the sudden Progress of that Rebellion, for indeed he was within a trifle of Ruin in that Affair; and had not the Crolians been deceiv'd by the darkness of the Night and led to a large Ditch of Water, which they could not pass over, they had certainly surpriz'd and overthrown his Army, and cut them in pieces, before they had known who had hurt them. Upon the Sense of this Danger, he takes up a pretence of necessity for the being always ready to resist the Factious Crolians, as he call'd them, and by that Insinuation hooks himself into a standing Army in time of Peace; - nay, and so easy were the Solunarian Church to yield up any point, which they did but imagin would help to crush their Brethren the Crolians, that they not only consented to this unusual Invasion of their antient Liberties, but sent up several Testimonials of their free Consent, nay, and of their Joy of having arriv'd to so great a Happiness, as to have a Prince that setting aside the formality of Laws would vouchsafe to Govern them by the glorious Method of a Standing Army. -

These Testimonials were things not much unlike our Addresses in England, and which when I heard I could not but remember our Case, in the time of the late King James, when the City of Carlisle in their Address, Thankt his Majesty for the Establishing a Standing Army in England in time of Peace, calling it the Strength, and Glory of the Kingdom.

So strong is the Ambition and Envy of Parties, these Solunarian Gentlemen not grudging to put out one of their own eyes, so they might at the same time put out both the Eyes of their Enemies; the Crolians rather consented to this badge of their own Slavery, and brought themselves who were a free People before, under the Power and Slavery of the Sword.

The ease with which this Prince got over so considerable a Point as this, made him begin to be too credulous and to perswade himself that the Solunarian Church-Men were really in earnest, as to their Pageant-Doctrin of Non-Resistance, and that as he had seen them bear with strange extravagancies on the Crolian Part, they were real and in earnest when they Preach'd that Men ought to obey for Conscience's sake, whatever hardship were impos'd upon them, and however unjust, or contrary to the Laws of God, Nature, Reason, or their Country; what Principle in the World could more readily prompt a Prince to attempt what he so earnestly coveted, as this zealous Prince did the restoring the Abrogratzian Faith, for since he had but two sorts of People to do with; one he had crush'd by force, and had brought the other to profess it their Religion, their Duty, and their Resolution to bear every thing he thought fit to Impose upon them, and that they should be Damn'd if they resisted, the Work seem'd half done to his Hand.

And indeed when I reflected on the Coherence of things, I could not so much blame this Prince for his venturing upon the probability, for whoever was but to go up to this Lunar World and read the Stories of that Time, with what Fury the hot Men of the Solunarian Church acted against the Dissenting Crolians, and with what warmth they assisted their Prince against them, and how Cruelly they insulted them after they were defeated in their attempt of Dethroning him, how zealously they Preach'd up the Doctrine of absolute undisputed Resignation to his Will, how frequently they obey'd several of his encroachments upon their Liberties, and what solemn Protestations they made to submit to him in any thing, and to stand by and assist him in whatever he Commanded them to the last Drop, much with the same Zeal and Forwardness, as our Life-and-Fortune Men did here in England. I say, when all this was consider'd, I could not so much condemn his Credulity, nor blame him for believing them, for no Man could have doubted their Sincerity, but he that at the same time must have Taxt them with most unexampled Hipocrisie.

For the Solunarians now began to discern their Prince was not really on their side, that neither in State Matters any more than Religion, he had any affection for them, and the first absolute Shock he gave them, was in Publishing a general Liberty to the Crolians. 'Tis true this was not out of respect to the Crolian Religion any more than the Solunarian, but purely because by that means he made way for an Introduction of the Abrogratzian Religion which now began to appear publickly in the Country.

But however, as this was directly contrary to the expectation of the Solunarians, it gave them such a disgust against their Prince, that from that very time being disappointed in the Soveraign Authority they expected, they entred into the deepest and blackest Conspiracy against their Prince and his Government that ever was heard of.

Many of the Crolians were deluded by the new Favour and Liberty they receiv'd from the Prince to believe him real, and were glad of the Mortification of their Brethren; but the more Judicious seeing plainly the Prince's Design, declar'd against their own Liberty, because given them by an illegal Authority, without the assent of the whole Body legally assembled.

When the Solunarians saw this they easily reconcil'd themselves to the Crolians, at least from the Outside of the Face, for the carrying on their Design, and so here was a Nation full of Plots, here was the Prince and his Abrogratzians plotting to introduce their Religion, here was a parcel of blind short-sighted Crolians plotting to ruin the Solunarian Establishment, and weakly joining with the Abrogratzians to satisfy their private Resentments; and here was the wiser Crolians joining heartily with the Solunarians of all sorts, laying aside private Resentments, and forgetting old Grudges about Religion, in order to ruin the invading Projects of the Prince and his Party.

There was indeed some verbal Conditions past between them, and the Solunarians willing to bring them into their Party promised them upon the Faith of their Nation, and the Honour of the Solunarian Religion, that there should be no more Hatred, Disturbance or Persecution for the sake of Religion between them, but that they would come to a Temper with them, and always be Brethren for the future. They declared that Persecution ran contrary to their Religion in general, and to their Doctrin in particular; and backt their Allegations with some Truths they have not since thought fit to like, nor much to regard.

However by this Artifice, and on these Conditions, they brought the Crolians to join with them in their Resolutions to countermine their designing Prince; these indeed were for doing it by the old way down-right, and to oppose Oppression with Force, a Doctrin they acknowledg'd, and profest to join with all the Lunar part of Mankind in the practice, and began to tell their Brethren how they had impos'd upon themselves and the World, in pretending to absolute Submission against Nature and universal Lunarian Practice.

But a cunning Fellow personating a Solunarian, and who was in the Plot, gravely answer'd them thus,

'Look ye, Gentlemen, we own with you that Nature, Reason, Law, Justice, and Custom of Nations is on your side, and that all Power Derives from, Centers in, and on all Recesses or Demises of Power returns to its Great Original the Party Governed: Nay we own our Great Eye from whom all the habitable Parts of this Globe are inlightned, has always directed us to practice what Nature thus dictates, always approv'd and generally succeeded the attempt of Dethroning Tyrants. But our Case differs, we have always pretended to this absolute undisputed Obedience, which we did indeed to gain the Power of your Party; and if we should turn round at once to your Opinion, tho' never so right, we should so fly in the Face of our own Doctrin, Sermons, innumerable Pamphlets and Pretensions, as would give all our Enemies too great a Power over us in Argument, and we should never be able to look Mankind in the Face: But we have laid our Measures so that by prompting the King to run upon us in all sorts of bare-fac'd Extreams and Violences, we shall bring him to exasperate the whole Nation; then we may underhand foment the breach on this side, raise the Mob upon him, and by acting on both sides seem to suffer a Force in falling in with the People, and preserve our Reputation.

'Thus we shall bring the thing to pass, betray our Prince, take Arms against his Power, call in Foreign Force to do the Work, and even then keep our Hands seemingly out of the Broil, by being pretended Sticklers for our former Prince; so save our Reputation, and bring all to pass with Ease and Calmness; while the eager Party of the Abrogratzians will do their own Work by expecting we will do it for them.

The Crolians astonish'd both at the Policy, the Depth, the Knavery and the Hypocrisy of the Design, left them to carry it on, owning it was a Masterpiece of Craft, and so stood still to observe the Issue, which every way answer'd the exactness of its Contrivance.

When I saw into the bottom of all this Deceit, I began to take up new Resolutions of returning back into our Old World again, and going home to England, where tho' I had conceiv'd great Indignation at the Treatment our Passive Obedience Men gave their Prince here, and was in hopes in these my remote Travels to have found out some Nations of Honour and Principles. I was fill'd with Amazement to see our Moderate Knaves so much out-done, and I was inform'd that all these things were meer Amusements, Vizors, and Shams, to bring an Innocent Prince into the Snare.

Would any Mortal imagin who has read this short Part of the Story, that all this was a Solunarian Church Plot, a meer Conspiracy between these Gentlemen and the Crolian Dissenters, only to wheedle in the unhappy Prince to his own Destruction, and bring the popular Advantage of the Mob, to a greater Ascendant on the Crown.

Of all the Richlieus, Mazarines, Gondamours, Oliver Cromwels, and the whole Train of Polititians that our World has produc'd, the greatest of their Arts are Follies to the unfathomable depth of these Lunarian Policies; and for Wheedle, Lying, Swearing, Preaching, Printing, &c. what is said in our World by Priests and Polititans, we thank God may be believ'd; but if ever I believe a Solunarian Priest Preaching Non-Resistance of Monarchs, or a Solunarian Polititian turning Abrogratzian, I ought to be mark'd down for a Fool; nor will ever any Prince in that Country take their Word again, if ever they have their Senses about 'em, but as this is a most extraordinary Scene, so I cannot omit a more particular and sufficient Relation of some Parts of it, than I us'd to give.

The Solunarian Clergy had carry'd on their Non-Resistance Doctrin to such Extremities, and had given this new Prince such unusual demonstrations of it, that he fell absolutely into the Snare, and entirely believ'd them; he had try'd them with such Impositions as they would never have born from any Prince in the World, nor from him neither, had they not had a deep Design, and consequently stood in need of the deepest Disguise imaginable; they had yielded to a Standing Army, and applauded it as a thing they had desir'd; they had submitted to levying Taxes upon them by New Methods, and illegal Practices; they had yielded to the abrogation or suspension at least of their Laws, when the King's absolute Will requir'd it; not that they were blind, and did not see what their Prince was doing, but that the black Design was so deeply laid, they found it was the only way to ruin him, to push him upon the highest Extreams, and then they should have their turn serv'd. - Thus if he desir'd one illegal Thing of them, they would immediately grant two; one would have thought they had read our Bible, and the Command, when a Man takes away the Cloak, to give him the Coat also.

Nor was this enough, but they seem'd willing to admit of the publick Exercise of the Abrogratzian Religion in all Parts; and when the Prince set it up in his own Chappel, they suffered it to be set up in their Cities, and Towns, and the Abrogratzian Clergy began to be seen up and down in their very Habits; a thing which had never been permitted before in that Country, and which the Common People began to be very uneasy at. But still the Solunarian Clergy, and all such of the Gentry, especially as were in the Plot, by their Sermons, printed Books, and publick Discourses, carry'd on this high topping Notion of absolute Submission, so that the People were kept under, and began to submit to all the impositions of the Prince.

These things were so acted to the Life, that not only the Prince, but none of his Abrogratzian Counsellors could see the Snare, the Hook was so finely covered by the Church-Artificers, and the Bait so delicious, that they all swallow'd it with eagerness and delight.

But the Conspirators willing to make a sure game of it, and not thinking the King, or all his Counsellors would drive on so fast as they would have them, tho' they had already made a fair progress for the Time, resolv'd to play home, and accordingly they persuade their Prince, that they will not only submit to his Arbitrary Will, in Matters of State, and Government, but in Matters of Religion; and in order to carry this Jest on, one of the heads of their Politicks, and a Person of great Estem for his Abilities in Matters of State, being without question one of the ablest Heads of all the Solunarian Nobility, pretended to be converted, and turn'd Abrogratzian. This immediately took as they desir'd, for the Prince caress'd him, and entertain'd him with all possible endearments, proferr'd him to several Posts of Honour and Advantage, always kept him near him, consulted him in all Emergencies, took him with him to the Abrogian Sacrifices, and he made no Scruple publickly to appear there, and by these degrees and a super-achitophalian Hypocrisie, so insinuated himself into the credulous Prince's favour, that he became his only Confident, and absolute Master of all his Designs.

Now the Plot had its desir'd effect, for he push'd the King upon all manner of Precipitations; and if even the Abrogratzians themselves who were about the King, interpos'd for more temperate Proceedings, he would call them Cowards, Strangers, ignorant of the Temper of the Lunarians, who when they were a going, might be driven, but if they were suffered to cool and consider, would face about and fall off.

Indeed the Men of Prudence and Estates among his own Party, I mean the Abrogratzians in the Country, frequently warn'd him to take more moderate Measures, and to proceed with more Caution; told him he would certainly ruin them all, and himself, and that there must be some Body about his Majesty that push'd him upon these Extremes, on purpose to set all the

Nation in a Flame, and to overthrow all the good Designs, which with Temper and good Conduct, might be brought to perfection.

Had these wary Councils been observ'd, and a Prudence and Policy agreeable to the mighty consequence of Things been practis'd, the Solunarian Church had run a great risque of being over thrown, and to have sunk gradually in the Abrogian Errors, the People began to be drawn off gradually, and the familiarity of the thing made it appear less frightful to unthinking People, who had entertain'd strange Notions of the monstrous things that were to be seen in it, so that common Vogue had fill'd the Peoples Minds with ignorant Aversions, that 'tis no absurdity to say, I believe there was 200000 People who would have spent the last drop of their Blood against Abrogratzianism, that did not know whether it was a Man or a Horse.

This thing consider'd well, would of it self have been sufficient to have made the Prince and his Friends wary, and to have taught them to suit their Measures to the Nature and Circumstances of Things before them; but Success in their beginnings blinded their Eyes, and they fell into this Church Snare with the most unpitied willingness that could be imagin'd.

The first thing therefore this new Counsellor put his Master upon, in order to the beginning his more certain Ruin, was to introduce several of his Abrograzians into Places of all kinds, both in the Army, Navy, Treasure, and Civil Affairs, tho' contrary to some of the general Constitutions of Government; he had done it into the Army before, tho' it had disgusted several of his Military Men, but now he push'd him upon making it

Universal, and still the Passive Solunarians bore it with patience.

From this tameness and submission, his next Step was to argue that he might depend upon it the Solunarian Church had so sincerely embrac'd the Doctrine of Non-Resistance, that they were now ripen'd not only to sit still, and see their Brethren the Crolians suppress'd, but to stand still and be opprest themselves, and he might assure himself the Matter was now ripe, he might do just what he wou'd himself with them, they were prepar'd to bare any thing.

This was the fatal Stroke, for having possest the Prince with the belief of this, he let loose the Reins to all his long conceal'd Desires. Down went their Laws, their Liberties, their Corporations, their Churches, their Colleges, all went to wreck, and the eager Abrograzians thought the Day their own. The Solunarians made no opposition, but what was contain'd within the narrow circumference of Petitions, Addresses, Prayers, and Tears; and these the Prince was prepar'd to reject, and upon all occasions to let them know he was resolv'd to be obey'd.

Thus he drove on by the treacherous Advice of his new Counsels, till he ripen'd all the Nation for the general Defection which afterward follow'd.

For as the Encroachments of the Prince push'd especially at their Church Liberties, and threatened the overthrow of all their Ecclesiastical Privileges, the Clergy no sooner began to feel that they were like to be the first Sacrifice, but they immediately threw off the Vizor, and beat the Concionazimir; this is a certain Ecclesiastick Engine which is usual in cases of general

Alarm, as the Churches Signal of Universal Tumult.

This is truly a strange Engine, and when a Clergy-Man gets into the Inside of it, and beats it, it Roars, and makes such a terrible Noise from the several Cavities, that 'tis heard a long way; and there are always a competent number of them plac'd in all Parts so conveniently, that the Alarm is heard all over the Kingdom in one Day.

I had some Thoughts to have given the Reader a Diagram of this piece of Art, but as I am but a bad Drafts Man, I have not yet been able so exactly to describe it, as that a Scheme can be drawn, but to the best of my Skill, take it as follows. 'Tis a hollow Vessel, large enough to hold the biggest Clergy-Man in the Nation; it is generally an Octagon in Figure, open before, from the Wast upward, but whole at the Back, with a Flat extended over it for Reverberation, or doubling the Sound; doubling and redoubling, being frequently thought necessary to be made use of on these occasions; 'tis very Mathematically contriv'd, erected on a Pedestal of Wood like a Windmil, and has a pair of winding Stairs up to it, like those at the great Tun at Hiedlebergh.

I could make some Hierogliphical Discourses upon it, from these References, thus.

1. That as it is erected on a Pedestal like a Wind-Mill, so it is no new thing for the Clergy, who are the only Persons permitted to make use of it, to make it turn round with the Wind, and serve to all the Points of the Compass.

2. As the Flat over it assists to encrease the Sound, by

forming a kind of hollow, or cavity proper to that purpose, so there is a certain natural hollowness, or emptiness, made use of sometimes in it, by the Gentlemen of the Gown, which serves exceedingly to the propogation of all sorts of Clamour, Noise, Railing, and Disturbance.

3. As the Stairs to it go winding up like those by which one mounts to the vast Tun of Wine at Hiedleburgh, which has no equal in our World, so the use made of these ascending Steps, is not altogether different, being frequently employ'd to raise People up to all sorts of Enthusiasms, spiritual Intoxications, mad and extravagant Action, high exalted Flights, Precipitations, and all kinds of Ecclesiastick Drunkenness and Excesses.

The sound of this Emblem of emptiness, the Concionazimir, was no sooner heard over the Nation, but all the People discover'd their readiness to join in with the Summons, and as the thing had been concerted before, they send over their Messengers to demand Assistance from a powerful Prince beyond the Sea, one of their own Religion, and who was allied by Marriage to the Crown.

They made their Story out so plain, and their King had by the contrivance of their Achitophel rendred himself so suspected to all his Neighbours, that this Prince, without any hesitation , resolv'd to join with them, and accordingly makes vast Preparations to invade their King.

During this interval their Behaviour was quite altred at home, the Doctrin of absolute Submission and Non-Resistance was heard no more among them, the Concionazimir beat daily to tell all the People they should stand up to Defend the Rights of the Church, and that it was time to look about them for the Abrograzians were upon them. The eager Clergy made this Ecclesiastick Engine sound as loud and make all the Noise they could, and no Men in the Nation were so forward as they to acknowledge that it was a State-Trick, and they were drawn in to make such a stir about the pretended Doctrins of absolute Submission, that they did not see the Snare which lay under it, that now their Eyes were opened, and they had learnt to see the Power and Superiority of Natural Right, and would be deceiv'd no longer. Others were so honest to tell the Truth, that they knew the emptiness and weakness of the pretence all along, and knew what they did when they Preacht it up, viz. to suppress and pull down the Crolians: But they thought their Prince who they always serv'd in crying up that Doctrin, and whose Exclusion was prevented by it, would ha' had more Gratitude, or at least more Sense, than to try the Experiment upon them, since whatever to serve his Designs and their own, which they always thought well united, they were willing to pretend, he could not but see they always knew better than to suffer the practice of it in their own Case. That since he had turn'd the Tables upon them, 'tis true he had them at an advantage and might pretend they were Knaves, and perhaps had an opportunity to call them so with some reason; but they were resolv'd, since he had drove them to the necessity of being one or t'other, tho' he might call them Knaves, they would take care he should have no reason to call them Fools too.

Thus the Vapour of absolute Subjection was lost on a suddain, and as if it had been preparatory to what was coming after, the Experiment was quickly made; for the King persuing his Encroachments upon the Church, and being possest with a Belief that pursuant to their open Professions they would submit to any thing, he made a beginning with them, in sending his positive Command to one of his Superintendent Priests, or Patriarchs, to forbid a certain Ecclesiastick to officiate any more till his Royal Pleasure was known.

Now it happen'd very unluckily that this Patriarch, tho' none of the most Learned of his Fraternity, yet had always been a mighty zealous Promoter of this blind Doctrin of Non-Resistance, and had not a little triumph'd over and insulted the Crolian Dissenters upon the Notion of Rebellion, antimonarchical Principles and Obedience, with a reserve for the Laws, and the like, as a scandalous practice, and comprehensive of Faction, Sedition, dangerous to the Church and State, and the like.

This Reverend Father was singl'd out as the first Mark of the King's Design; the deluded Prince believ'd he could not but comply, having so publickly profest his being all Submission and absolute Subjection; but as this was all Conceit, he was pusht on to make the Assault where he was most certain to meet a repulse; and this Gentleman had long since thrown off the Mask, so his first Order was disobey'd.

The Patriarch pretended to make humble Remonstrances, and to offer his Reasons why he could not in Conscience, as he call'd it, comply. The King, who was now made but a meer Engine, or Machine, screw'd up or down by this false Counsellor to act his approaching Destruction with his own Hand, was prompted to resent this Repulse with the utmost Indignation, to reject all manner of Submissions, Excuses or Arguments, or any thing but an immediate, absolute compliance, according to the Doctrin so often inculcated; and this he run on so high, as to put the Patriarch in Prison for Contumacy.

The Patriarch as absolutely refus'd to submit, and offer'd himself to the Decision of the Law.

Now it was always a sacred Rule in these Lunar Countries, that both King and People are bound to stand by the arbitrimnet of the Law in all Cases of Right or Claim, whether publick or private; and this has been the reason that all the Princes have endeavour'd to cover their Actions with pretences of Law, whatever really has been in their Design; for this reason the King could not refuse to bring the Patriarch to a Tryal, where the Humour of the People first discover'd it self, for here Passive Obedience was Try'd and Cast, the Law prov'd to be superior to the King, the Patriarch was acquitted, his Disobedience to the King justify'd, and the King's Command prov'd unjust.

The Applause of the Patriarch, the Acclamations of the People, and the general Rejoycings of the whole Nation at this Transaction, gave a black prospect to the Abrograzians; and a great many of them came very honestly and humbly to the King and told him, if he continued to go on by these Measures he would ruin them all; they told him what general Alarm had been over the whole Nation by the Clamours of the Clergy; and the beating of the Concionazimir in all Parts, inform'd him how the Doctrin of absolute Obedience was ridicul'd in all Places, and how the Clergy began to preach it back again like a Witches Prayer, and that it would infallibly raise the Devil of Rebellion in all the Nation, they besought him to content himself with the liberty of their Religion, and the freedom they enjoy'd of being let into Places and Offices of Trust and Honour, and to wait all reasonable Occasions to encrease their Advantages, and gradually to gain Ground; they entreated him to consider the impossibility of reducing so mighty, so obstinate, and so resolute a Nation all at once. They pleaded how rational a thing it was to expect that by Degrees and good Management, which by precipitate Measures would be endanger'd and overthrown.

Had these wholsome Counsels taken place in the King's Mind he had been King to his last hour, and the Solunarians and Crolians too had been all undone, for he had certainly incroach'd upon them gradually, and brought that to pass in time which by precipitant Measures he was not likely to effect.

It was therefore a master-piece of Policy in the Solunarian Church-men to place a feign'd Convert near their Prince, who shou'd always biass him with contrary Advices, puff him up with vast prospect of Success, prompt him to all Extreams, and always Fool him with the certainty of bringing Things to pass his own way.

These Arts made him set light by the repulse he met with in the Matter of the Patriarch, and now he proceeds to make two Attacks more upon the Church; one was by putting some of his Abrograzian Priests into a College among some of the Solunarian Clergy; and the other was to oblige all the Solunarian Clergy to read a certain Act of his Council, in which his Majesty admitted all the Abrograzians, Crolians, and all sorts of Dissenters, to a freedom of their Religious Exercises, Sacrifices, Exorcisms, Dippings, Preachings, &c. and to prohibit the Solunarians to Molest or Disturb them.

Now as this last was a bitter reproach to the Solunarian Church for all the ill Treatment the Dissenting Crolians had receiv'd from them, and as it was exprest in the Act that all such Treatment was Unjust and Unchristian, so for them to read it in their Temples, was to acknowledge that they had been guilty of most unjust and irreligious Dealings to the Crolians, and that their Prince had taken care to do them Justice.

The matter of introducing the Abrograzians into the Colleges or Seminaries of the Solunarian Priests, was actually against the Sacred Constitutions and Foundation Laws of those Seminaries.

Wherefore in both these Articles they not only disobey'd their Prince, but they oppos'd him with those trifling Things call'd Laws, which they had before declar'd had no Defensive Force against their Prince; these they had recourse to now, insisted upon the Justice and Right devolv'd upon them by the Laws, and absolutely refus'd their compliance with his Commands.

The Prince, pusht upon the Tenters before, receiv'd their Denial with exceeding Resentment, and was heard with deep regret, to break out in Exclamations at their unexpected faithless Proceedings, and sometimes to express himself thus: Horrid Hypocrisy! Surprizing Treachery! Is this the absolute Subjection which in such numerous Testimonials or Addresses you profest, and for which you so often and so constantly branded the poor Crolians, and told me that your Church was wholly made up of Principles of Loyalty and Obedience! But I'll be fully satisfied for this Treatment.

In the minute of one of those Excursions of his Passion, came into his Presence the seemingly revolted Lunarian Noble Man, and falling in with his present Passions, prompts him to a speedy revenge; and propos'd his erecting a Court of Searches, something like the Spanish Inquisition, giving them plenipotentiary Authority to hear and determine all Ecclesiastical Causes absolutely, and without Appeal.

He empower'd these Judges to place by his absolute Will, all the Abrograzian Students in the Solunarian College, and tho' they might make a formal Hearing for the sake of the Form, yet that by Force it should be done.

He gave them Power to displace all those Solunarian Clergy-Men that had refus'd to read his Act of Demission to the Abrograzian, and Crolian Dissenters, and 'twas thought he design'd to keep their Revenues in Petto, till he might in time fill them up to some of his own Religion.

The Commission accordingly began to act, and discovering a full Resolution to fulfil his Command, they by Force proceeded with the Students of the Solunarian College; and it was very remarkable, that even some of the Solunarian Patriarchs were of this number, who turn'd out their Brethren the Solunarian Students, to place Abrograzians in their room.

This indeed they are said to have repented of since, but however, these it seems were not of the Plot, and therefore did not foresee what was at hand.

The rest of the Patriarchs who were all in the Grand Design, and saw things ripening for its Execution, upon the apprehension of this Court of Searches beginning with them, make an humble Address to their Prince, containing the Reasons why they could not comply with his Royal Command.

The incens'd King upbraided them with his having been told by them of their absolute and unreserv'd Obedience, and refusing their Submissions or their Reasons, sent them all to Jail, and resolv'd to have brought them before his new High Court of Searches, in order, as was believ'd, to have them all displac'd.

And now all began to be in a Flame, the Sollicitations of the Solunarian Party, having obtain'd powerful Relief Abroad, they began to make suitable preparations at Home. The Gentry and Nobility who the Clergy had brought to join with them, furnish'd themselves with Horses and Arms, and prepar'd with their Tenants and Dependants to join the Succours as soon as they should Arrive.

In short, the Forreign Troops they had procur'd, Arriv'd, Landed, and publish'd a long Declaration of all the Grievances which they came to redress.

No sooner was this Forreign Army arriv'd with the Prince at the head of them, but the face of Affairs altred on a suddain. The King indeed, like a brave Prince, drew all his Forces together, and marching out of his Capital City, advanced above 500 Stages, things they measure Land with in those Countries, and much about our Furlong, to meet his Enemy.

He had a gallant Army well appointed and furnish'd, and all things much superior to his Adversary, but alas the Poison of Disobedience was gotten in there, and upon the first March he offer'd to make towards the Enemy one of his great Captains with a strong Party of his Men went over and revolted.

This Example was applauded all over the Nation, and by this time one of the Patriarchs, even the same mention'd before that had so often preacht Non-Resistance of Princes, lays by his Sacred Vestments, Mitre, and Staff, and exchanging his Robes for a Soldier's Coat, mounts on Horseback, and in short, appears in Arms against his Lord. - Nor was this all, but the Treacherous Prelate takes along with him several Solunarian Lords, and Persons of the highest Figure, and of the Houshold, and Family of the King, and with him went the King's own Daughter, his principle Favourites and Friends.

At the News of this, the poor deserted Prince lost all Courage, and abandoning himself to Despair, he causes his Army to retreat without fighting a Stroke, quits them and the Kingdom at once, and takes Sanctuary with such as could escape with him, in the Court of a Neighbouring Prince.

I have heard this Prince exceedingly blam'd, for giving himself up to Despair so soon. - That he thereby abandon'd the best and faithfullest of his Friends, and Servants, and left them to the Mercy of the Solunarians; that when all these that would have forsaken him were gone, he had Forces equal to his Enemies; that his Men were in Heart, fresh and forward; that he should have stood to the last; retreated to a strong Town, where his Ships rod, and which was over against the Territories of his great Allie, to whom he might have deliver'd up the Ships which were there, and have thereby made him Superior at Sea to his

Enemies, and he was already much Superior at Land; that there he might have been reliev'd with Forces too strong for them to match, and at least might have put it to the issue of a fair Battle. - Others, that he might have retreated to his own Court, and capital City, and taking possession of the Citadel, which was his own, might so have aw'd the Citizens who were infinitely Rich, and Numerous, with the apprehensions of having their Houses burnt, they would not have dar'd to have declar'd for his Enemies, for fear of being reduc'd to heaps and ruins; and that at last he might have set the City on Fire in 500 Places, and left the Solunarian Church-Men a Token to remember their Non-Resisting Doctrine by, and yet have made an easy Retreat down the Harbour, to other Forts he had below, and might with ease have destroy'd all the Shipping, as he went.

'Tis confess'd had he done either, or both these things, he had left them a dear bought Victory, but he was depriv'd of his Counsellor, for as soon as things came to this height, the Achitophel we have so often mention'd, left him also, and went away; all his Abrograzian Priests too fosook him, and he was so bereft of Counsel that he fell into the Hands of his Enemies as he was making his escape, but he got away again, not without the connivance of the Enemy, who were willing enough he should go; so he got a Vessel to carry him over to the Neighbouring Kingdom, and all his Armies, Ships, Forts, Castles, Magazines, and Treasure, fell into his Enemies Hands.

The Neighbouring Prince entertain'd him very kindly, Cherish'd him, Succour'd him, and furnish'd him with Armies and Fleets for the recovery of his Dominions, which has occasion'd a tedious War with that Prince, which continues to this Day.

Thus far Passive Doctrins, and Absolute Submission serv'd a Turn, bubl'd the Prince, wheedled him in to take their Word who profess'd it, 'till he laid his Finger upon the Men themselves, and that unravell'd all the Cheat; they were the first that call'd in Forreign Power, and took up Arms against their Prince.

Nor did they end here, but all this Scene being over, and the Forreign Prince having thus deliver'd them, and their own King being thus chas'd away, the People call themselves together, and as Reason good, having been deliver'd by him from the Miseries, Brangles, Oppressions, and Divisions of the former Reign, they thought they could do no less than to Crown their Deliverer; and having Summon'd a general Assembly of all their Capital Men, they gave the Crown to this Prince who had so generously sav'd them.

And here again I heard the first King exceedingly blam'd for quitting his Dominions, for had he staid here, tho' he had actually been in their Hands, unless they wou'd have Murther'd him, they could never have proceeded to the Extremeties they did reach to, nor cou'd they ever have Crown'd the other Prince, he being yet alive and in his own Dominions.

But by quitting the Country, they fix'd a legal Period to their Obedience, he having deserted their Protection, and Defence, and openly laid down the Administration.

But as these sort of Politicks cannot be decided by us, unless we know the Constitutions of those Lunar Regions, so we cannot pretend to make a Decision of what might, or might not have happen'd.

It remains to examine how those Solunarians behav'd

themselves, who had so earnedly cryed up the Principles of Obedience, and absolute Submission.

Nothing was so Ridiculous, now they saw what they had done, they began to repent, and upon recollection of Thoughts some were so asham'd of themselves, that having broken their Doctrin, and being now call'd upon to tranfpose their Allegiance, truly they stopt in the mid-way, and so became Martyrs on both sides.

I can liken these to nothing so well as to those Gentlemen of our English Church, who tho' they broke into the Principles of Passive Obedience by joining, and calling over the P. of O. yet suffer'd deprivations of Benefices, and loss of their Livings, for not taking the Oath; as if they had not as effectually perjur'd themselves by taking up Arms against their King, and joyning a Forreign Power, as they could possibly do afterward, by Swearing to live quietly under the next King.

But these nice Gentlemen are infinitely outdone in these Countries, for these Solunarians by a true Church turn, not only refuse to transpose their Allegiance, but pretend to wipe their Mouths as to former taking Arms, and return to their old Doctrins of absolute Submission, boast of Martyrdom, and boldly reconcile the contraries of taking up Arms, and Non-Resistance, charging all their Brethren with Schism, Rebellion, Perjury, and the damnable Sin of Resistance.

Nor is this all, for as a great many of these Solunarian Church-Men had no affection to this new Prince, but were not equally furnished, or qualify'd for Martyrdom with their Brethren; they went to certain Wise Men, who being cunning at splitting Hairs, and making distinctions, might perhaps furnish them with some mediums between Loyalty and Disloyalty; they apply'd themselves with great dilligence to these Men, and they by deep Study, and long Search, either found or made the quaintest Device for them that ever was heard of.

By this unheard of Discovery, to their great Joy and Satisfaction, they have arriv'd at a Power, which all the Wise Men in our World could never pretend to, and which 'tis thought, could the description of it be regularly made, and brought down hither, would serve for the Satisfaction and Repose of a great many tender Consciences, who are very uneasy at Swearing to save their Benefices.

These great Makers of Distinction, have learn't to distinguish between active Swearing, and passive Swearing, between de facto Loyalty, and de jure Loyalty, and by this decent acquirement they obtain'd the Art of reconciling Swearing Allegiance without Loyalty, and Loyalty without Swearing, so that native and original Loyalty may be preserv'd pure and uninterrupted, in spight of all subsequent Oaths, to prevailing Usurpations.

Many are the Mysteries, and vast the Advantages of this new invented Method, Mental Reservations, Inuendoes, and Double Meanings are Toys to this, for they may be provided for in the litteral terms of an Oath, but no Provision can be made against this; for these Men after they have taken the Oath, make no Scruple to declare, they only Swear to be quiet, as long as they can make no Disturbance; that they are left liberty still to espouse the Interest and Cause of their former Prince, they nicely distinguish between

Obedience and Submission, and tell you a Slave taken into Captivity, tho' he Swears to live peaceably, does not thereby renounce his Allegiance to his natural Prince, nor abridge himself of a Right to attempt his own Liberty if ever opportunity present.

Had these neat Distinctions been found out before, none of our Solunarian Clergy, no not the Patriarchs themselves surely would have stood out, and suffer'd such Depredations on their Fortunes and Characters as they did; they wou'd never have been such Fools to have been turn'd out of their Livings for not Swearing, when they might have learnt here that they might have swore to one Prince, and yet have retain'd their Allegiance to another; might have taken an Oath to the new, without impeachment of their old Oaths to the absent Prince. - It is great pity these Gentlemen had not gone up to the Moon for Instruction in this difficult Case.

There they might have met with excellent Logicians, Men of most sublime Reasons, Dr. Overall, Dr. Sherlock, and all our nice Examiners of these things wou'd appear to be no Body to them; for as the People in these Regions have an extraordinary Eye-sight, and the clearness of the Air contributs much to the help of their Opticks, so they have without doubt a proportion'd clearness of discerning, by which they see as far into Mill-stones, and all sorts of Solids, as the nature of things will permit, but above all, their Faculties are blest with two exceeding Advantages.

1. With an extraordinary distinguishing Power, by which they can distinguish even Indivisibles, part Unity it self, divide Principles, and distinguish Truth into such and so many minute Particles, till they

dwindle it away into a very Nose of Wax, and mould it into any Form they have occasion for, by which means they can distinguish themselves into or out of any Opinion, either in Religion, Politicks or Civil Right, that their present Emergencies may call for.

2. Their reasoning Faculties have this further advantage, that upon occasion they can see clearly for themselves, and prevent others from the same discovery, so that when they have occasion to see any thing which presents for their own Advantage, they can search into the Particulars, make it clear to themselves, and yet let it remain dark and mysterious to all the World besides. Whether this is perform'd by their exceeding Penetration, or by casting an artificial Veil over the Understandings of the Vulgar, Authors have not yet determin'd; but that the Fact is true, admits of no Dispute.

And the wonderful Benefit of these Things in point of Dispute is extraordinary, for they can see clearly they have the better of an Argument, when all the rest of the World think they have not a Word to say for themselves: 'Tis plain to them that this or that proves a thing, when Nature, by common Reasoning, knows no such Consequences.

I confess I have seen some weak Attempts at this extraordinary Talent, particularly in the Disputes in England between the Church and the Dissenter, and between the High and Low Church, wherein People have tollerably well convinc'd themselves when no Body else could see any thing of the Matter, as particularly the famous Mr. W - ly about the Antimonarchical Principles taught in the Dissenters Accademies; ditto in L - sly, about the Dissenters burning the City, and setting Fire to their own Houses to destroy their Neighbours; and another famous Author, who prov'd that Christopher Love lost his Head for attempting to pull down Monarchy by restoring King Charles the Second.

These indeed are some faint Resemblances of what I am upon; but alas! these are tender sort of People, that han't obtain'd a compleat Victory over their Consciences, but suffer that Trifle to reproach them all the while they are doing it, to rebel against their resolv'd Wills, and check them in the middle of the Design; from which Interruptions arise Palpitations of the Heart, Sickness and squeamishness of Stomach; and these have proceeded to Castings and Vomit, whereby they have been forc'd sometimes to throw up some such unhappy Truths as have confounded all the rest, and flown in their own Faces so violently, as in spight of Custom has made them blush and look downward; and tho' in kindness to one another they have carefully lickt up one anothers Filth, yet this unhappy squeamishness of Stomach has spoil'd all the Design, and turn'd the Appetites of their Party, to the no small prejudice of a Cause that stood in need of more Art and more Face to carry it on as it shou'd be with a thoro'-pac'd Case-harden'd Policy, such as I have been relating, is compleatly obtain'd in these Regions, where the Arts and Excellencies of sublime Reasonings are carried up to all the extraordinaries of banishing Scruples, reconciling Contradictions, uniting Opposites, and all the necessary Circumstances requir'd in a compleat Casuist.

'Tis not easily conceivable to what extraordinary Flights they have carry'd this strength of Reasoning, for besides the distinguishing nicely between Truth and

Error, they obtain a most refin'd Method of distinguishing Truth it self into Seasons and Circumstances, and so can bring any thing to be Truth, when it serves the turn that happens just then to be needful, and make the same thing to be false at another time.

And this method of circumstantiating Matters of Fact into Truth or Falshood, suited to occasion, is found admirably useful to the solving the most difficult Phanomena of State, for by this Art the Solunarian Church made Persecution be against their Principles at one time, and reducible to Practice at another. They made taking up Arms, and calling in Foreign Power to depose their Prince, consistent with Non-Resistance, and Passive Obedience; nay they went farther, they distinguisht between a Crolian's taking Arms, and a Solunarians, and fairly prov'd this to be Rebellion and that to be Non-Resistance.

Nay, and which exceeded all the Power of human Art in the highest degrees of Attainment that ever it arriv'd to on our side the Moon; they turn'd the Tables so dexterously, as to argument upon one sort of Crolians, call'd Prestarians; that tho' they repented of the War they had rais'd in former Times, and protested against the violence offer'd their Prince; and after another Party had in spight of them Beheaded him, took Arms against the other Party, and never left contriving their Ruin, till they had brought in his Son, and set him upon the Throne again.

Yet by this most dextrous way of Twisting, Extending, Contracting, and Distinguishing of Phrases and Reasoning, they presently made it as plain as the Sun at Noon Day; that these Prestarians were King-killers, Common-wealths Men, Rebels, Traytors, and Enemies to Monarchy; that they restor'd the Monarchy only in order to Destroy it, and that they Preach'd up Sedition, Rebellion and the like: This was prov'd so plain by these sublime Distinctions, that they convinc'd themselves and their Posterity of it, by a rare and newly acquir'd Art, found out by extraordinary Study, which proves the wonderful power of Custom, insomuch, that let any Man by this method, tell a Lye over a certain number of times, he shall arrive to a Satisfaction of its certainty, tho' he knew it to be a Fiction before, and shall freely tell it for a Truth all his life after.

Thus the Prestarians were call'd the Murtherers of the Father, tho' they restor'd the Son, and all the Testimonials of their Sufferings, Protests and Insurrections to prevent his Death, signify'd nothing, for this method of Distinguishing has that powerful Charm in it, that all those Trifles we call Proofs and Demonstration were of no use in that Case. Custom brought the Story up to a Truth, and in an instant all the Crolians were hookt in under the general Name of Prestarians, at the same time to hook all Parties in the Crime.

Now as it happen'd at last that these Solunarian Gentlemen found it necessary to do the same thing themselves, viz. To lay aside their Loyalty, Depose, Fight against, shoot Bullets at, and throw Bombs at their King till they frighted him away, and sent him abroad to beg his Bread. The Crolians began to take Heart and tell them, now they ought to be Friends with them, and tell them no more of Rebellion and Disloyalty; nay, they carry'd it so far as to challenge them to bring their Loyalty to the Test, and compare Crolian Loyalty and Solunarian Loyalty together, and see who had rais'd more Wars, taken up Arms oftenest, or appear'd in most Rebellions against their Kings; nay, who had kill'd most Kings, the Crolians or the Solunarians, for there having been then newly fought a great Battle between the Solunarian Church-Men under their new Prince, and the Armies of Foreign Succours under their old King, in which their old King was beaten and forc'd to flie a second time, the Crolians told them that every Bullet they shot at the Battle was as much a murthering their King, as cutting off the Head with a Hatchet was a killing his Father.

These Arguments in our World would have been unanswerable, but when they came to be brought to the Test of Lunar Reasoning, alas they signify'd nothing; they distinguisht and distinguisht till they brought the Prestarian War to be meer Rebellion, King-killing, Bloody and Unnatural; and the Solunarian fighting against their King, and turning him adrift to seek his Fortune, no prejudice at all to their Loyalty, no, nor to the famous Doctrine of Passive Obedience and Absolute Subjection.

When I saw this, I really bewail'd the unhappiness of some of our Gentlemen in England, who standing exceedingly in need of such a wonderful Dexterity of Argument to defend their share in our late Revolution, and to reconcile it to their anticedent and subsequent Conduct, should not be furnish'd from this more accurate World with the suitable Powers, in order the better to defend them against the Banter and just Raillery of their ill-natur'd Enemies the Whigs.

By this they might have attained suitable reserves of Argument to distinguish themselves out of their Loyalty, and into their Loyalty, as occasion presented to dismiss this Prince, and entertain that, as they found it to their purpose; but above all, they might have learnt a way how to justify Swearing to one King and Praying for another, Eating one Prince's Bread and doing another Prince's Work, Serving one King they don't Love and Loving another they don't Serve; they might easily reconcile the Schisms of the Church, and prove they are still Loyal Subjects to King James, while they are only forc'd Bonds-Men to the Act of Settlement, for the sake of that comfortable Importance, call'd Food and Rainment; and thus their Reputation might have been sav'd, which is most unhappily tarnish'd and blur'd, with the malicious Attacks of the Whigs on one Hand, and the Non-Jurants on the other.

These Tax them as above with Rebellion by their own Principles, and contradicting the Doctrin of Passive Submission and Non-Resistance, by taking up Arms against their Prince, calling in a Foreign Power, and deposing him: They charge them with killing the Lord's Anointed, by Shooting at him at the Boyn, where if he was not kill'd it was his own fault, at least 'tis plain 'twas none of theirs.

On the other Hand, the Non Jurant Clergy charge them with Schism, declare the whole Church of England Schismaticks, and breakers off from the general Union of the Church, in renouncing their Allegiance, and Swearing to another Power, their former Prince being yet alive.

'Tis confest all the Answers they have been able to make to these things, are very weak and mean, unworthy Men of their Rank and Capacities, and 'tis pity they should not be assisted by some kind

Communication of these Lunar Arguments and Distinctions, without which, and till they can obtain which, a Conforming Jacobite must be the absurdest Contradiction in Nature; a thing that admits of no manner of Defence, no, not by the People themselves, and which they would willingly abandon, but that they can find no side to join with them.

The Dissenting Jacobites have some Plea for themselves, for let their Opinion be never so repugnant to their own Interest, or general Vogue, they are faithful to some thing, and they wont joyn with these People, because they have Perjur'd their Faith, and yet pretend to adhere to it at the same time. The Conforming Whigs won't receive them, because they pretend to rail at the Government they have Sworn to, and espouse the Interest they have Sworn against; so that these poor Creatures have but one way left them, which is to go along with me, next time I Travel to the Moon, and that will most certainly do their Business, for when they come down again, they will be quite another sort of Men, the Distinctions, the Power of Argument, the way of Reasoning, they will be then furnish'd with will quite change the Scene of the World with them, they'll certainly be able to prove they are the only People, both in Justice, in Politicks and in Prudence; that the extremities of every side are in the Wrong, they'll prove their Loyalty preserv'd, untainted, thro' all the Swearings, Fightings, Shootings and the like, and no Body will be able to come to the Test with them; so that upon the whole, they are all distracted if they don't go up to the Moon for Illumination, and that they may easily do in the next Consolidator.

But as this is a very long Digression, and for which I am to beg my Reader's Pardon, being an Error I slipt into from my abundant respect to these Gentlemen, and for their particular Instruction, I shall endeavour to make my Reader amends, by keeping more close to my Subject.

To return therefore to the Historical part of the Solunarian Church-Men, in the World in the Moon.

Having as is related Depos'd their King, and plac'd the Crown upon the Head of the Prince that came to their assistance, a new Scene began all over the Kingdom.

1. A terrible and bloody War began thro' all the parts of the Lunar World, where their banish'd Prince and his new Allie had any Interest; and the new King having a universal Character over all the Northern Kingdoms of the Moon, he brought in a great many Potent Kings, Princes, Emperors and States, to take part with him, and so it became the most general War that had happen'd in those Ages.

I did not trouble my self to enquire into the particular Successes of this War, but at what had a more particular regard to the Country from whence I came, and for whose Instruction I have design'd these Sheets, the Strife of Parties, the Internal Feuds at home, and their Analogy to ours; and whatever is instructively to be deduced from them, was the Subject of immediate Inquiry.

No sooner was this Prince plac'd on the Throne, but according to his Promises to them that invited him over, he conven'd the Estates of the Realm, and giving them free Liberty to make, alter, add or repeal, all such Laws as they thought fit, it must be their own fault if they did not Establish themselves upon such

Foundation of Liberty, and Right, as they desir'd; for he gave them their full Swing, never interpos'd one Negative upon them for several Years, and let them do almost every thing they pleas'd.

This full Liberty had like to have spoil'd all, for as is before noted, this Nation had one unhappy Quality they could never be broke of, always to be falling out one among another.

The Crolians, according to Capitulation, demanded the full Liberty and Toleration of Religion, which the Solunarians had condition'd with them for, when they drew them off from joyning with the old King, and when they promis'd to come to a Temper, and to be Brethren in Peace and Love ever after.

Nor were the Solunarian Church-Men backward, either to remember, or perform the Conditions but by the consent of the King, who had been by agreement made Guarantee of their former Stipulations, an Act was drawn up in full Form, and as compleat, as both satisfy'd the desires of the Crolians, and testify'd the Honesty and Probity of the Solunarians, as they were abstractedly and moderately consider'd.

During the whole Reign of this King, this Union of Parties continu'd without any considerable Interruption, there was indeed brooding Mischiefs which hovered over every accident, in order to generate Strife, but the Candor of the Prince, and the Prudence of his Ministers, kept it under for a long time.

At last an occasion offer'd it self, which gave an unhappy Stroke to the Nation's Peace. The King thro' innumerable Hazards, terrible Battles and a twelve

Years War, had reduc'd his powerful Adversary to such a necessity of Peace, that he became content to abandon the fugitive King, and to own the Title of this Warlike Prince; and upon these, among various other Conditions, very Honourable for him, and his Allies, and by which vast Conquests were surrendred, and disgorg'd to the Losers, a Peace was made to the Universal Satisfaction of all those Parts of the Moon that had been involv'd in a tiresome and expensive War.

This Peace was no sooner made, but the Inhabitants of this unhappy Country, according to the constant Practice of the Place, fell out in the most horrid manner among themselves, and with the very Prince that had done all these great things for them; and I cannot forget how the Old Gentleman I had these Relations from, being once deeply engag'd in Discourse with some Senators of that Country, and hearing them reproach the Memory of that Prince from whom they receiv'd so much, and on the foot of whose Gallantry and Merit the Constitution then subsisted, it put him into some heat, and he told them to their Faces that they were guilty both of Murther and Ingratitude.

I thought the Charge was very high, but as they return'd upon him, and challeng'd him to make it out, he answer'd he was ready to do it, and went on thus.

His Majesty, said he, left a quiet, retir'd, compleatly happy Condition, full of Honour, belov'd of his Country, Vallu'd and Esteem'd, as well as Fear'd by his Enemies, to come over hither at your own Request, to deliver you from the Encroachments and Tyranny as you call'd it, of your Prince.

Ever since he came hither, he has been your meer Journy-Man, your Servant, your Souldier of Fortune, he has Fought for you, Fatigu'd and Harras'd his Person, and rob'd himself of all his Peace for you; he has been in a constant Hurry, and run thro' a Million of Hazards for you; he has convers'd with Fire and Blood, Storms at Sea, Camps and Trenches ashore, and given himself no rest for twelve Years, and all for your Use, Safety and Repose: In requital of which, he has been always treated with Jealousies, and Suspitions, with Reproaches, and Abuses of all Sorts, and on all Occasions, till the ungrateful Treatment of the Solunarians eat into his very Soul, tir'd it with serving an unthankful Nation, and absolutely broke his Heart; for which reason I think him as much Murther'd as his Predecessor was, whose Head was cut off by his Subjects.

I could not when this was over, but ask the Old Gentlemen, what was the reason of his Exclamation, and how it was the People treated their Prince upon this occasion?

He told me it was a grievous Subject, and a long one, and too long to rehearse, but he would give me a short Abridgment of it; and not to look back into his Wars, in which he was abominably ill serv'd, his subjects constantly ill treated him in giving him Supplies too late, that he cou'd not get into the Field, nor forward his Preparations in time to be ready for his Enemies, who frequently were ready to insult him in his Quarters.

By giving him sham Taxes and Funds, that raised little or no Mony, by which he having borrow'd Mony of his People by Anticipation, the Funds not answering, he contracted such vast Debts as the Nation could never Pay which brought the War into disrepute, sunk the Credit of his Exchequer, and fill'd the Nation with Murmurs and Complaint.

By betraying his Counsel and well laid Designs to his Enemies, selling their Native Country to Foreigners, retarding their Navies and Expeditions, till the Enemies were provided to receive them, betraying their Merchants and Trade, spending vast Sums to fit out Fleets, just time enough to go Abroad, and do nothing, and then get Home again.

But as these were too numerous Evils, and too long to repeat, the particular things he related to in his Discourse, were these that follow.

There had been a hasty Peace concluded with a furious and powerful Enemy, the King foresaw it would be of no continnuace, and that the demise of a neighbouring King, who by all appearance could not live long, would certainly embroil them again. - He saw that Prince keep up numerous Legions of Forces, in order to be in a posture to break the Peace with advantage. This the King fairly represented to them, and told them the necessity of keeping up such a Force, and for such a Time, at least as might be necessary to awe the Enemy from putting any affront upon them in case of the Death of that Prince, which they daily expected.

The Party who had all along malign'd the Prosperity of this Prince, took fire at the Offer, and here began another State Plot, which tho' it hookt in two or three sets of Men for different Ends, yet altogether join'd in affronting and ill treating their Prince, upon this Article of the Army.

The Nation had been in danger enough from the designs of former Princes invading their Priviledges, and putting themselves in a Posture to Tyrannize by the help of standing Forces, and the Party that first took Fire at this Proposal tho' the very same Men who in the time of an Abrogratzian Prince, were for caressing him, and giving him Thanks for his Standing Army, as has been noted before, were the very People that began the outcry against this Demand, and so specious were the Pretences they made, that they drew in the very Crolians themselves upon the pretence of Liberty, and Exemption from Arbitrary Methods of Government to oppose their King.

It griev'd this good Prince to be suspected of Tyrannick Designs, and that by a Nation who he had done so much, and ventur'd so far to save from Tyranny, and Standing Armies; 'twas in vain he represented to them the pressing occasion; in vain he gave them a Description of approaching Dangers, and the threatning posture of the Enemies Armies; in vain he told them of the probabilities of renewing the War, and how keeping but a needful Force might be a means of preventing it; in vain he propos'd the subjecting what Force should be necessary to the Absolute Power, both as to Time and Number of their own Cortez or National Assembly.

It was all one, the Design being form'd in the Breasts of those who were neither Friends to the Nation, nor the King, those Reasons which would have been of Force in another Case, made them the more eager; bitter Reflections were made on the King, and scurrilous Lampoons publish'd upon the Subject of Tyrants, and Governing by Armies.

Nothing could be more ungrateful to a generous Prince, nor could any thing more deeply affect this King, than whom none ever had a more genuine, single-hearted Design for the Peoples good, but above all, like Casar in the Case of Brutus, it heartily mov'd him to find himself push'd at by those very People whom he had all along seen, pretending to adhere to his Interest, and the Publick Benefit, which he had always taken care should never be parted, and to find these People join against this Proposal, as a Design against their Liberties, and as a Foundation of Tyranny heartily and sensibly afflicted him.

It was a strange Mistery, and not easily unriddled, that those Men who had always a known aversion to the Interest of the depos'd King should fall in with this Party, and those that were Friends to the general Good, never forgave it them.

All that could be said to excuse them, was the Plot I am speaking of, that by carrying this Point for that Party, they hookt in those forward People to join in a popular Cry of Liberty and Property, things they were never fond of before, and to make some Settlement of the Peoples Claims which they always had oppos'd, and which they would since have been very glad to have repeal'd.

So great an Ascendant had the Personal Spleen of this Party over their other Principles, that they were content to let the Liberties of the People be declar'd in their highest Claims, rather than not obtain this one Article, which they knew would so exceedingly mortify their Prince, and strengthen the Nations Enemies. They freely join'd in Acts of Succession, Abjuration, Declaration of the Power and Claims of the People, and the Superiority of their Right to the Princes Prerogative, and abundance of such things, which they could never be otherwise brought to.

'Tis true these were great things, but 'twas thought all this might have been obtain'd in Conjunction with their Prince, rather than by putting Affronts and Mortifications upon the Man that had next to the Influence of Heaven been the only Agent of restoring them to a Power and Capacity of enjoying, as well as procuring, such things as National Priviledges.

'Twas vigorosly alledg'd that Standing Armies in times of Peace, were inconsistent with the Publick Safety, the Laws and Constitutions of all the Nations in the Moon.

But these Allegations were strenuously answer'd, that it was true without the consent of the great National Council, it was so, but that being obtain'd, it was not illegal, and publick Necessities might make that consent, not only legal, but convenient.

'Twas all to no purpose, the whole was carry'd with a Torrent of Clamour and Reflection against the good Prince, who consented, because he would in nothing oppose the Current of the People; but withal, told them plainly what would be the consequences of their Heat, which they have effectually found true since to their Cost, and to the loss of some Millions of Treasure.

For no sooner was this Army broke, which was the best ever that Nation saw, and was justly the Terror of the Enemy, but the great Monarch we mention'd before, broke all Measures with this Prince and the Confederate Nations, a Proof what just apprehensions they had of his Conduct, at the head of such an Army. For they broke with contempt, a Treaty which the Prince upon a prospect of this unkindness of his People had entred into with the Enemy, and which he engag'd in, if possible, to prevent a new War, which he foresaw he should be very unfit to begin, or carry on, and which they would never have dar'd to break had not this Feud happen'd.

It was but a little before I came into this Country, when such repeated Accounts came, of the Incroachments, Insults and Preparations of their great powerful Neighbour, that all the World saw the necessity of a War, and the very People who were to feel it most apply'd to the Prince to begin it.

He was forward enough to begin it, and in compliance with his People, resolv'd on it; but the Grief of the usage he had receiv'd, the unkind Treatment he had met with from those very People that brought him thither, had sunk so deep upon his Spirits, that he could never recover it; but being very weak in Body and Mind, and join'd to a slight hurt he receiv'd by a fall from his Horse, he dyed, to the unspeakable grief of all his Subjects that wish'd well to their Native Country.

This was the melancholly Account of this great Prince's end, and I have been told that at once every Year, there is a kind of Fast, or solemn Commemoration kept up for the Murther of that former Prince, who, as I noted, was Beheaded by his Subjects; So it seems some of the People, who are of Opinion this Prince was Murther'd by the ill Treatment of his Friends, a way which I must own, is the cruellest of Deaths, keep the same Day, to commemorate his Death, and this is a Day, in which it seems both Parties are very free with one another, as to Rallery and ill Language.

But the Friends of this last Prince have a double advantage, for they also commemorate the Birth Day of this Prince, and are generally very merry on that Day; and the custom is at their Feast on that Day, just like our drinking Healths, they pledge one another to the immortal Memory of their Deliverer; as the Historical part of this Matter was absolutely necessary to introduce the following Remarks, and to instruct the Ignorant in those things, I hope it shall not be thought a barren Digression, especially when I shall tell you that it is a most exact Representation of what is yet to come in a Scene of Affairs, of which I must make a short Abstract, by way of Introduction.

The deceas'd Prince we have heard of, was succeeded by his Sister in-Law, the second Daughter of the banish'd Prince, a Lady of an extraordinary Character, of the Old Race of their Kings, a Native by Birth, a Solunarian by Profession; exceeding Pious, Just and Good, of an Honesty peculiar to her self, and for which she was justly belov'd of all sorts and degrees of her Subjects.

This Princess having the Experience of her Father and Grand-father before her, join'd to her own Prudence and Honesty of Design; it was no wonder if she prudently shun'd all manner of rash Counsels, and endeavour'd to carry it with a steady Hand between her contending Parties.

At her first coming to the Crown, she made a solemn Declaration of her resolutions for Peace and just Government; she gave the Crolians her Royal Word, that she would inviolably preserve the Toleration of their Religion and Worship, and always afford them her Protection, and by this she hop'd they would be easy.

But to the Solunarians, as those among whom she had been Educated, and whose Religion she had always profess'd, been train'd up in, and Piously persued; she express'd her self with an uncommon Tenderness, told them they should be the Men of her Favour, and those that were most zealous for that Church should have most of her Countenance; and she back'd this soon after with an unparallel'd Act of Royal Bounty to them, freely parting with a considerable Branch of her Royal Revenue, for the poor Priests of that Religion, of which there were many in the remote Parts of her Kingdom.

What vast Consequences, and prodigiously differing from the Design, may Words have when mistaken and misayplyed by the Hearers. Never were significant Expressions spoken from a sincere, honest and generous Principle, with a single Design to ingage all the Subjects in the Moon, to Peace and Union, so perverted, misapply'd and turn'd by a Party, to a meaning directly contrary to the Royal Thoughts of the Queen: For from this very Expression, most Zealous, grew all the Divisions and Subdivisions in the Solunarian Church, to the Ruin of their own Cause, and the vast advantage of the Crolian Interest. The eager Men of the Church, especially those we have been talking of, hastily catch'd at this Expression of the Queen, Most Zealous, and Millions of fatal Constructions , and unhappy Consequences they made of it, some of which are as follows.

1. They took it to imply that the Queen whatever she

had said to the Crolians, really design'd their Destruction, and that those that were of that Opinion, must be meant by the Most Zealous Members of the Solunarian Church, and they could understand Zeal no otherwise than their own way.

2. From this Speech, and their mistaking the Words Most Zealous, arose an unhappy Distinction among the Solunarians themselves, some Zealous, some More Zealous, which afterwards divided them into two most opposite Parties, being fomented by an accident of a Book publish'd on an Occasion, of which presently.

The Consequences of this mistake, appear'd presently in the Most Zealous, in their offering all possible Insults to the Crolian Dissenters, Preaching them down, Printing them down, and Talking them down, as a People not fit to be suffer'd in the Nation, and now they thought they had the Game sure.

Down with the Crolians began to be all the Cry, and truly the Crolians themselves began to be uneasy, and had nothing to rely upon but the Queens Promise, which however her Majesty always made good to them.

The other Party proceeded so far, that they begun to Insult the very Queen her self, upon the Matter of her Word, and one of her College-Priests told her plainly in Print, she could not be a true Friend to the Solunarian Church, if she did not declare War against, and root out all the Crolians in her Dominions.

But these Proceedings met with a Check, by a very odd accident: A certain Author of those Countries, a very mean, obscure and despicable Fellow, of no great share of Wit, but that had a very unlucky way of telling his Story, seeing which way things were a going, writes a Book, and Personating this high Solunarian Zeal, musters up all their Arguments, as if they were his own, and strenuously pretends to prove that all the Crolians ought to be Destroy'd, Hang'd, Banish'd, and the D - l and all. As this Book was a perfect Surprize to all the Country, so the Proceedings about it on all sides were as extraordinary.

The Crolians themselves were surpriz'd at it, and so closely had the Author couch'd his Design, that they never saw the irony of the Stile, but began to look about them, to see which way they should fly to save themselves.

The Men of Zeal we talk'd of, were so blinded with the Notion which suited so exactly with their real Design, that they hugg'd the Book, applauded the unknown Author, and plac'd the Book next their Oraclar Writings, or Laws of Religion.

The Author was all this while conceal'd, and the Paper had all the effect he wish'd for.

For as it caus'd these first Gentlemen to caress, applaud and approve it, and thereby discover'd their real Intention, so it met with Abhorrence and Detestation in all the Men of Principles, Prudence and Moderation in the Kingdom, who tho' they were Solunarians in Religion, yet were not for Blood, Desolation and Persecution of their Brethren, but with the Queen were willing they should enjoy their Liberties and Estates, they behaving themselves quietly and peaceably to the Government.

At last it came out that it was writ by a Crolian; but good God! What a Clamour was rais'd at the poor Man, the Crolians flew at him like Lightning, ignorantly and blindly, not seeing that he had sacrific'd himself and his Fortunes in their behalf; they rumag'd his Character for Reproaches, tho' they could find little that way to hurt him; they plentifully loaded him with ill Language and Railing, and took a great deal of pains to let the World see their own Ignorance and Ingratitude.

The Ministers of State, tho' at that time of the fiery Party, yet seeing the general Detestation of such a Proposal, and how ill it would go down with the Nation, tho' they approv'd the thing, yet began to scent the Design, and were also oblig'd to declare against it, for fear of being thought of the same Mind.

Thus the Author was Proscrib'd by Proclamation, and a Reward of 50000 Hecato's, a small imaginary Coin in those Parts, put upon his Head.

The Cortez of the Nation being at the same time assembled join'd in Censuring the Book, and thus the Party blindly damn'd their own Principles for meer shame of the practice, not daring to own the thing in publick which they had underhand profest, and the fury of all Parties fell upon the poor Author.

The Man fled the first popular Fury, but at last being betraid fell into the Hands of the publick Ministry.

When they had him they hardly knew what to do with him; they could not proceed against him as Author of a Proposal for the Destruction of the Crolians because it appear'd he was a Crolian himself; they were loth to charge him with suggesting that the Solunarian Church-men were guilty of such a Design, least he should bring their own Writings to prove it true; so they fell to wheadling him with good Words to throw himself into their Hands and submit, giving him that Geu-gau the Publick Faith for a Civil and Gentleman-like Treatment; the Man, believing like a Coxcomb that they spoke as they meant, quitted his own Defence, and threw himself on the Mercy of the Queen as he thought; but they abusing their Queen with false Representations, Perjur'd all their Promises with him, and treated him in a most barbarous manner, on pretence that there were no such Promises made, tho' he prov'd it upon them by the Oath of the Persons to whom they were made.

Thus they laid him under a heavy Sentence, Fin'd him more than they thought him able to pay, and order'd him to be expos'd to the Mob in the Streets.

Having him at this Advantage they set upon him with their Emissaries to discover to them his Adherents, as they call'd them, and promis'd him great Things on one Hand, threatning him with his utter Ruin on the other; and the Great Scribe of the Country, with another of their great Courtiers, took such a low Step as to go to him to the Dungeon where they had put him, to see if they could tempt him to betray his Friends. The Comical Dialogue between them there the Author of this has seen in Manuscript, exceeding diverting, but having not time to Translate it 'tis omitted for the present; tho' he promises to publish it in its proper Season for publick Instruction.

However for the present it may suffice to tell the World, that neither by promises of Reward or fear of

Punishment they could prevail upon him to discover any thing, and so it remains a Secret to this day.

The Title of this unhappy Book was The shortest way with the Crolians. The Effects of it were various, as will be seen in our ensuing Discourse: As to the Author nothing was more unaccountable than the Circumstances of his Treatment; for he met with all that Fate which they must expect who attempt to open the Eyes of a Nation wilfully blind.

The hot Men of the Solunarian Church damn'd him without Bell, Book, or Candle; the more Moderate pitied him, but lookt on as unconcern'd: But the Crolians, for whom he had run this Venture, us'd him worst of all; for they not only abandon'd him, but reproacht him as an Enemy that would ha' them destroy'd: So one side rail'd at him because they did understand him, and the other because they did not.

Thus the Man sunk under the general Neglect, was ruin'd and undone, and left a Monument of what every Man must expect that serves a good Cause, profest by an unthankful People.

And here it was I found out that my Lunar Philosopher was only so in Disguise, and that he was no Philosopher, but the very Man I have been talking of.

From this Book, and the Treatment its Author receiv'd, for they us'd him with all possible Rigour, a new Scene of Parties came upon the Stage, and this Queen's Reign began to be fill'd with more Divisions and Feuds than any before her.

These Parties began to be so numerous and violent that

it endanger'd the Publick Good, and gave great Disadvantages to the general Affairs abroad.

The Queen invited them all to Peace and Union, but 'twas in vain; nay, one had the Impudence to publish that to procure Peace and Union it was necessary to suppress all the Crolians, and have no Party but one, and then all must be of a Mind.

From this heat of Parties all the moderate Men fell in with their Queen, and were heartily for Peace and Union: The other, who were now distinguish'd by the Title of High Solunarians, call'd these all Crolians and Low Solunarians, and began to Treat them with more Inveteracy than they us'd to do the Crolians themselves, calling them Traytors to their Country, Betrayers of their Mother, Serpents harbour'd in the Bosom, who bite, sting and hiss at the Hand that succour'd them; and in short the Enmity grew so violent, that from hence proceeded one of the subtilest, foolishest, deep, shallow Contrivances and Plots that ever was hatcht or set on foot by any Party of Men in the whole Moon, at least who pretended to any Brains, or to half a degree of common Understanding.

There had always been Dislikes and Distasts between even the most moderate Solunarians and the Crolians, as I have noted in the beginning of this Relation, and these were deriv'd from Dissenting in Opinions of Religion, ancient Feuds, private Interest, Education, and the like; and the Solunarians had frequently, on pretence of securing the Government, made Laws to exclude the Crolians from any part of the Administration, unless they submitted to some Religious Tests and Ceremonies which were prescrib'd them.

Now as the keeping them out of Offices was more the Design than the Conversion of the Crolians to the Solunarian Church, the Crolians, at least many of them, submitted to the Test, and frequently Conform'd to qualify themselves for publick Employments.

The most moderate of the Solunarians were in their Opinion against this practice, and the High Men taking advantage of them, drew them in to Concur in making a Law with yet more Severity against them, effectually to keep them out of Employment.

The low Solunarians were easy to be drawn into this Project, as it was only a Confirming former Laws of their own making, and all Things run fair for the Design; but as the High Men had further Ends in it than barely reducing the Crolians to Conformity, they coucht so many gross Clauses into their Law, that even the Grandees of the Solunarians themselves could not comply with; nay even the Patriarchs of the Solunarian Church declar'd against it, as tending to Persecution and Confusion.

This Disappointment enrag'd the Party, and that very Rage entirely ruin'd their Project; for now the Nobility, the Patriarchs, and all the wise Men of the Nation, joining together against these Men of Heat and Fury, the Queen began to see into their Designs, and as she was of a most pious and peaceable Temper, she conceiv'd a just Hatred of so wicked and barbarous a Design, and immediately dismiss'd from her Council and Favour the Great Scribe, and several others who were Leaders in the Design, to the great mortification of the whole Party, and utter Ruin of the intended Law against the Crolians.

Here I could not but observe, as I have done before in the Case of the banish'd King, how impolitick these high Solunarian Church-men acted in all their Proceedings, for had they contented themselves by little and little to ha' done their Work, they had done it effectually; but pushing at Extremities they overshot themselves, and ruin'd all.

For the Grandees and Patriarchs made but a few trifling Objections at first, nay and came off, and yielded some of them too; and if these would ha' consented to ha' parted with some Clauses which they have willingly left out since, they had had it pass'd; but these were as hot Men always are, too eager and sure of their Game, they thought all was their own, and so they lost themselves.

If they rail'd at the low Solunarian Church-men before, they doubled their Clamors at them now, all the Patriarchs, and all the Nobility and Grandees, nay even the Queen her self came under their Censure, and every Body who was not of their Mind were Prestarians and Crolians.

As this Rage of theirs was implacable, so, as I hinted before, it drove them into another Subdivision of Parties, and now began the Mysterious Plot to be laid which I mention'd before; for the Cortez being summon'd, and the Law being proposed, some of these high Solunarians appear'd in Confederacy with the Crolians, in perfect Confederacy with them, a thing no Body would have imagin'd could ever ha' been brought to pass.

Now as these sorts of Plots must always be carry'd very nicely, so these high Gentlemen who

Confederated with the Crolians, having, to spight the other, resolv'd effectually to prevent the passing the Law against the Qualification of the Crolians, it was not their Business immediately to declare themselves against it as a Law, but by still loading it with some Extravagance or other, and pushing it on to some intolerable Extreme, secure its miscarriage.

In the managing this Plot, one of their Authors was specially employ'd, and that all that was really true of the Crolian Dissenters might be ridicul'd, his Work was to draw monstrous Pictures of them, which no Body could believe; this took immediately, for now People began to look at their Shooes to see if they were not Cloven Footed as they went a long Streets; and at last finding they were really shap'd like the rest of the Lunar Inhabitants, they went back to the Author, who was a Learned Member of a certain Seminary, or Brother-hood of the Solunarian Clergy, and enquir'd if he were not Mad, Distracted and Raving, or Moon-blind, and in want of the thinking Engine; but finding all things right there, and that he was in his Senses, especially in a Morning when he was a little free from, &c. that he was a Good, Honest, Jolly, Solunarian Priest, and no room could be found for an Objection there. Upon all these Searches it presently appear'd, and all Men concluded it was a meer Fanatick Crolian Plot; that this High Party of all were but Pretenders, and meer Traytors to the True High Solunarian Church-Men, that wearing the same Cloth had herded among them in Disguise, only to wheedle them into such wild Extravagancies as must of necessity confuse their Councils, expose their Persons, and ruin their Cause. - According to the like Practice, put upon their Abrograzian Prince, and of which I have spoken before.

And since I am upon the detection of this most refin'd Practice, I crave leave to descend to some particular Instances, which will the better evince the Truth of this Matter, and make it appear that either this was really a Crolian Plot, or else all these People were perfectly Distracted; and as their Wits in that Lunar World, are much higher strain'd than ours, so their Lunacy, where it happens, must according to the Rules of Mathematical Nature, bear an extream Equal in proportion.

This College Fury of a Man was the first on whom this useful Discovery was made, and having writ several Learned Tracts wherein he invited the People to Murther and Destroy all the Crolians, Branded all the Solunarian Patriarchs, Clergy and Gentry that would not come into his Proposal, with the name of Cowards, Traytors and Betrayers of Lunar Religion; having beat the Concionazimir at a great Assembly of the Cadirs, or Judges, and told them all the Crolians were Devils, and they were all Perjur'd that did not use them as such: He carry'd on Matters so dexterously, and with such surprizing Success, that he fill'd even the Solunarians themselves with Horror at his Proposals. - And as I happen'd to be in one of their publick Halls where all such Writings as are new are laid a certain time to be read by every Comer, I saw a little knot of Men round a Table, where one was reading this Book.

There were two Solunarian High Priests in their proper Vestments, one Privy Councellor of the State, one other Noble Man, and one who had in his Hat a Token, to signifie that he possest one of the fine Feathers of the Consolidator, of which I have given the Description already.

The Book being read by one of the habited Priests, he starts up with some warmth, by the Moon, says he, I have found this Fellow out, he is certainly a Crolian, a meer Prestarian Crolian, and is crept into our Church only in Disguise, for 'tis certain all this is but meer Banter and Irony to expose us, and to ridicule the Solunarian Interest.

The Privy Councellor took it presently, whether he is a Crolian or no, says he, I cannot tell, but he has certainly done the Crolians so much Service, that if they had hir'd him to act for them, they could not have desir'd he should serve them better.

Truly, says the Man of the Feather, I was always for pulling down the Crolians, for I thought them dangerous to the State; but this Man has brought the Matter nearer to my View, and shown me what destroying them is, for he put me upon examining the Consequences, and now I find it would be lopping off the Limbs of the Government, and laying it at the Mercy of the Enemy that they might lop off its Head; I assure you he has done the Crolians great Service, for whereas abundance of our Men of the Feather were for routing the Crolians, they lately fell down to 134 or thereabouts.

All this confirm'd the first Man's Opinion that he was a Crolian in Disguise, or an Emissary employ'd by them to ruin the Project of their Enemies; for these Crolians are damn'd cunning People in their way, and they have Mony enough to engage Hirelings to their side.

Another Party concern'd in this Plot was an old cast-out Solunarian Priest, who, tho' professing himself a Solunarian, was turn'd out for adhering to the

Abrograzian King, a mighty Stickler for the Doctrin of absolute Subjection.

This Man draws the most monstrous Picture of a Crolian that could be invented, he put him in a Wolf's Skin with long Asses Ears, and hung him all over full of Associations, Massacres, Persecutions, Rebellions, and Blood. Here the People began to stare again, and a Crolian cou'd not go along the Street but they were alway's looking for the long Ears, the Wolf's Claws, and the like; 'till at last nothing of these Things appearing, but the Crolians looking and acting like other Folks, they begun to examine the Matter, and found this was a meer Crolian Plot too, and this Man was hir'd to run these extravagant lengths to point out the right meaning.

The Discovery being made, People ever since understand him that when he talks of the Dissenters Associations, Murthers, Persecutions, and the like, he means that his Readers should look back to the Murthers, Oppressions and Persecutions they had suffered for several past years, and the Associations that were now forming to bring them into the same Condition again.

From this famous Author I could not but proceed to observe the farther Progress of this most refin'd piece of Cunning, among the very great Ones, Grandees, Feathers, and Consolidators of the Country. For these Cunning Crolians manag'd their Intriegues so nicely, that they brought about a Famous Division even among the High Solunarian Party themselves; and whereas the Law of Qualification was reviv'd again, and in great Danger of being compleated; these subtle Crolians brought over One Hundred and Thirty Four of the Feathers in the Famous Consolidator to be of their side, and to Contrive the utter Destruction of it; and thus fell the Design which the High Solunarian Church Men had laid for the Ruin of the Crolians Interest, by their own Friends first joyning in all the Extremes they had proposed, and then pushing it so much farther, and to such mad Periods that the very highest of them stood amaz'd at the Design, startled, flew back and made a full stop; they were willing to Ruin the Crolians, but they were not willing to Ruin the whole Nation. The more these Men began to consider, the more furiously these Plotters carry'd on their Extravagances; at last they made a General push at a thing in which they knew if the other High Men joyn'd, they must throw all into Confusion, bring a Foreign Enemy on their Backs, unravel all the Thread of the War, fight all their Victories back again, and involve the whole Nation in Blood and Confusion.

They knew well enough that most of the High Men would hesitate at this, they knew if they did not the Grandees and Patriarchs would reject it, and so they plaid the surest Game to blast and overthrow this Law, that could possibly be plaid.

If any Man, in the whole World in the Moon, will pretend this was not a Plot, a Crolian Design, a meer Conspiracy to destroy the Law, let him tell me for what other end could these Men offer such extreams as they needs must know would meet with immediate opposition, things that they knew all the Honest Men, all the Grandees, all the Patriarchs, and almost all the Feathers would oppose.

From hence all the Men of any fore-sight brought it to this pass, as is before Noted, that either these One

Hundred and Thirty Four were Fools or Mad-Men, or that it was a Phanatick Crolian Plot and Conspiracy to Ruin the makeing this Law, which the rest of the Solunarian Church Men were very forward to carry on.

I heard indeed some Men Argue that this could not be, the breach was too wide between the Crolians and these Gentlemen ever to come to such an Agreement; but the Wiser Heads who argu'd the other way, always brought them, as is noted above, to this pinch of Argument; that either it must be so, be a Fanatick Crolian Plot, or else the Men of Fury were all Fools, Madmen, and fitter for an Hospital, than a State-House, or a Pulpit.

It must be allow'd, these Crolians were Cunning People, thus to wheedle in these High Flying Solunarians to break the Neck of their dear Project.

But upon the whole, for ought I cou'd see, whether it went one way or t'other, all the Nation esteem'd the other People Fools - Fools of the most extraordinary Size in all the Moon, for either way they pull'd down what they had been many Years a Building.

I cannot say that this was in kindness to the Crolians, but in meer Malice to the Low Solunarian Party, who had the Government in their Hands, for Malice always carries Men on to monstrous Extremes.

Some indeed have thought it hard to call this a Plot, and a Confederacy with the Crolians. - But I cannot but think it the kindest thing that can be said of them, and that 'tis impossible those People who push'd at some imaginary Things in that Law could but be in a Plot as aforesaid , or be perfectly Lunatick, down right

Mad-Men, or Traytors to their Country, and let them choose which Character they like.

I cannot in Charity but spare them their Honesty, and their Senses, and attribute it all to their Policy.

When I had understood all things at large, and found the exceeding depth of the Design; I must confess the Discovery of these things was very diverting, and the more so, when I made the proper Reflections upon the Analogy there seem'd to be between these Solunarian High Church-Men in the Moon, and ours here in England; our High Church-Men are no more to compare to these, than the Hundred and Thirty Four, are to the Consolidators.

Ours can Plot now and then a little among themselves, but then 'tis all Gross and plain Sailing, down right taking Arms, calling in Foreign Forces, Assassinations and the like; but these are nothing to the more Exquisite Heads in the Moon. For they have the subtillest Ways with them, that ever were heard of. They can make War with a Prince, on purpose to bring him to the Crown; fit out vast Navies against him, that he may have the more leisure to take their Merchant Men; make Descents upon him, on purpose to come Home and do nothing; if they have a mind to a Sea Fight, they carefully send out Admirals that care not to come within half a Mile of the Enemy, that coming off safe they may have the boasting Part of the Victory, and the beaten Part both together.

'Twould be endless to call over the Roll of their sublime Politicks. They damn Moderation in order to Peace and Union, set the House on Fire to save it from Desolation, Plunder to avoid Persecution, and consolidate Things in order to their more immediate Dissolution.

Had our High Church-Men been Masters of these excellent Arts, they had long ago brought their Designs to pass.

The exquisite Plot of these High Solunarians answer'd the Crolians End, for it broke all their Enemies Measures, the Law vanish'd, the Grandees could hardly be perswaded to read it, and when it was propos'd to be read again, they hist at it, and threw it by with Contempt.

Nor was this all; for it not only lost them their Design as to this Law, but it also absolutely broke the Party, and just as it was with Adam and Eve, as soon as they Sinn'd they Quarrell'd, and fell out with one another; so, as soon as things came to this height, the Party fell out one among another, and even the High Men themselves were divided, some were for Consolidating, and some not for Consolidating, some were for Tacking, and some not for Tacking, as they were, or were not let into the Secret.

If this Confusion of Languages, or Interest, lost them the real Design, it cannot be a wonder; have we not always seen it in our World, that dividing an Interest, weakens and exposes it? Has not a great many both good and bad Designs been render'd Abortive in this our Lower World, for want of the Harmony of Parties, and the Unanimity of those concern'd in the Design?

How had the knot of Rebellion been dissolv'd in England, if it had not been untied by the very Hands of those that knit it? All the contrary Force had been entirely broken and subdu'd, and the Restoration of Monarchy had never happen'd in England, if Union and Agreement had been found among the managers of that Age.

The Enemies of the present Establishment have shown sufficiently that they perfectly understand the shortest way to our infallible Destruction, when they bend their principle Force at dividing us into Parties, and keeping those parties at the utmost variance.

But this is not all, the Author of this cannot but observe here that as England is unhappily divided among Parties, so it has this one Felicity even to be found in the very matter of her Misfortunes, that those Parties are all again subdivided among themselves.

How easily might the Church have crusht and subdu'd the Dissenters if they had been all as mad as one Party, if they had not been some High and some Low Church-men. And what Mischief might not that one Party ha' done in this Nation, had not they been divided again into Jurant Jacobites and Non-Jurant, into Consolidators and Non-Consolidators? From whence 'tis plain to me, that just as it is in the Moon these Consolidating Church-men are meer Confederates with the Whigs; and it must be so, unless we should suppose them meer mad Men that don't know what they are a doing, and who are the Drudges of their Enemies, and kno' nothing of the Matter.

And from this Lunar Observation it presently occur'd to my Understanding, that my Masters the Dissenters may come in for a share among the Moon-blind Men of this Generation, since had they done for their own Interest what the Laws fairly admits to be done, had they been united among themselves, had they form'd themselves into a Politick Body to have acted in a publick, united Capacity by general Concert, and as Persons that had but one Interest and understood it, they had never been so often Insulted by every rising Party, they had never had so many Machines and Intrigues to ruin and suppress them, they had never been so often Tackt and Consolidated to Oppression and Persecution, and yet never have rebell'd or broke the Peace, incurr'd the Displeasure of their Princes, or have been upbraided with Plots, Insurrections and Antimonarchical Principles; when they had made Treaties and Capitulations with the Church for Temper and Toleration, the Articles would have been kept, and these would have demanded Justice with an Authority that would upon all Occasions be respected.

Were they united in Civil Polity in Trade and Interest, would they Buy and Sell with one another, abstract their Stocks, erect Banks and Companies in Trade of their own, lend their Cash to the Government in a Body, and as a Body.

If I were to tell them what Advantages the Crolians in the Moon make of this sort of management, how the Government finds it their Interest to treat them civilly, and use them like Subjects of Consideration; how upon all Occasions some of the Grandees and Nobility appear as Protectors of the Crolians, and treat with their Princes in their Names, present their Petitions, and make Demands from the Prince of such Loans and Sums of Mony as the publick Occasions require; and what abundance of Advantages are reapt from such a Union, both to their own Body as a Party, and to the Government also they would be convinc'd; wherefore I cannot but very earnestly desire of the Dissenters and

Whigs in my own Country that they would take a Journy in my Consolidator up to the Moon, they would certainly see there what vast Advantages they lose for want of a Spirit of Union, and a concert of Measures among themselves.

The Crolians in the Moon are Men of large Souls, and Generously stand by one another on all Occasions; it was never known that they deserted any Body that suffer'd for them, my Old Philosopher excepted, and that was a surprize upon them.

The Reason of the Difference is plain, our Dissenters here have not the Advantage of a Cogitator, or thinking Engine, as they have in the Moon. - We have the Elevator here and are lifted up pretty much, but in the Moon they always go into the Thinking Engine upon every Emergency, and in this they out-do us of this World on every Occasion.

In general therefore I must note that the wisest Men I found in the Moon, when they understood the Notes I had made as above, of the sub-divisions of our Parties, told me that it was the greatest Happiness that could ha' been obtained to our Country, for that if our Parties had not been thus divided, the Nation had been undone. They own'd that had not their Solunarian Party been divided among themselves, the Crolians had been undone, and all the Moon had been involv'd in Persecution, and been very probably subjected to the Gallunarian Monarch.

Thus the fatal Errors of Men have their advantages, the seperate ends they serve are not foreseen by their Authors and they do good against the very Design of the People, and the nature of the Evil it self.

And now that I may encourage our People to that Peace and good Understanding among themselves, which can alone produce their Safety and Deliverance; I shall give a brief Account how the Crolians in the Moon came to open their Eyes to their own Interest, how they came to Unite; and how the Fruits of that Union secur'd them from ever being insulted again by the Solunarian Party, who in time gave over the vain and fruitless Attempt, and so a universal Lunar Calm has spread the whole Moon ever since.

If our People will not listen to their own Advantages, nor do their own Business, let them take the consequences to themselves, they cannot blame the Man in the Moon.

To endeavour to bring this to pass, as these Memoirs have run thro' the general History of the Feuds and unhappy Breaches between the Solunarian Church and the Crolian Dissenters in the World of the Moon, it would seem an imperfect and abrupt Relation, if I should not tell you how, and by what Method, tho' long hid from their Eyes, the Crolians came to understand their own Interest and know their own Strength.

'Tis true, it seem'd a Wonder to me when I consider'd the Excellence and Variety of those perspective Glasses I have mentioned, the clearness of the Air, and consequently of the Head, in this Lunar World. I say it was very strange the Crolians should ha' been Moon Blind so long as they were, that they could not see it was always in their Power if they had but pursued their own Interest, and made use of those, legal Opportunities which lay before them, to put themselves in a Posture, as that the Government it self should think them a Body too big to be insulted, and find it their Interest to keep Measures with them.

It was indeed a long time before they open'd their Eyes to these advantages, but bore the Insults of the hair-brain'd Party, with a weakness and negligence that was as unjustifiable in them, as unaccountable to all the Nations of the Moon.

But at last, as all violent Extremes rouze their contrary Extremeties, the folly and extravagance of the High Solunarians drove the Crolians into their Senses, and rouz'd them to their own Interest, the occasion was among a great many others as follows.

The eager Solunarian could not on all occasions forbear to show their deep Regret at the Dissenting Crolians enjoying the Tolleration of their Religion, by a Law - .

And when all their legal Attempts to lessen that Liberty had prov'd Abortive, her Solunarian Majesty on all Occasions repeating her assurances of the continuance of her Protection, and particularly the maintaining this Tolleration Inviolable. They proceeded then to show the remains of their Mallice, in little Insults, mean and illegal Methods, and continual private Disturbances upon particular Persons, in which, however the Crolians having recourse to the Law, always found Justice on their side, and had redress with Advantage, of which the following Instance is more than ordinarily Remarkable.

There had been a Law made by the Men of the Feather, that all the meaner Idle sort of People, who had no settel'd way of living should go to the Wars, and the Lazognians, a sort of Magistrates there, in the nature of our Justices of the Peace, were to send them away by Force.

Now it happen'd in a certain Solunarian Island, that for want of a better, one of their High Priests was put into the Civil Administration, and made a Lazognian. - In the Neighbourhood of this Man's Jurisdiction, one of their own Solunarian Priests had turn'd Crolian, and whether he had a better Tallent at performance, or rather was more diligent in his Office is not material, but he set up a kind of a Crolian Temple in an old Barn, or some such Mechanick Building, and all the People flock'd after him.

This so provok'd his Neighbours of the black Girdle, an Order of Priests, of which he had been one, that they resolv'd to suppress him let it cost what it would.

They run strange lengths to bring this to pass.

They forg'd strange Stories of him, defam'd him, run him into Jayl upon frivolous and groundless Occasions, represented him as a Monster of a Man, told their Story so plain, and made it so specious, that even the Crolians themselves to their Shame, believ'd it, and took up Prejudices against the Poor Man, which had like to ha' been his Ruin.

They proscrib'd him in Print for Crimes they could never prove, they branded him with Forgery, Adultery, Drunkenness, Swearing, breaking Jayl, and abundance of Crimes; but when Matters were examin'd and things came to the Test, they could never prove the least thing upon him. - In this manner however they continually worryed the poor Man, till they ruin'd his Family and reduc'd him to Beggary; and tho' he came out of the

Prison they cast him into by the meer force of Innocence, yet they never left persuing him with all sorts of violence. - At last they made use of their Brother of the Girdle who was in Commission as above, and this Man being High Priest and Lazonian too, by the first was a Party, and by the last had a Power to act the Tragedy they had plotted against the poor Man.

In short, they seiz'd him without any Crime alledg'd, took violently from him his Licence, as a Crolian Priest, by which the Law justify'd what he had done, pretending it was forg'd, and after very ill Treating him, condemn'd him to the Wars, delivers him up for a Souldier, and accordingly carry'd him away.

But it happen'd, to their great Mortification, that this Man found more Mercy from the Men of the Sword, than from those of the Word, and so found means to get out of their Hands, and afterwards to undeceive all the Moon, both as to his own Character, and as to what he had Suffer'd.

For some of the Crolians, who began to be made sensible of the Injury done the poor Man, advis'd him to have recourse to the Law, and to bring his Adversaries before the Criminal Bar.

But as soon as this was done, good God! what a Scene of Villainy was here opened: The poor Man brought up such a Cloud of Witnesses to confront every Article of their Charge, and to vindicate his own Character, that when the very Judges heard it, tho' they were all Solunarians themselves, they held up their Hands, and declar'd in open Court it was the deepest Track of Villany that ever came before them, and that the

Actors ought to be made Examples to all the Moon.

The Persons concern'd, us'd all possible Arts to avoid, or at least to delay the Shame, and adjourn the Punishment, thinking still to weary the poor Man out. - But now his Brethren the Crolians began to see themselves wounded thro' his Sides, and above all, finding his Innocence clear'd up beyond all manner of dispute, they espous'd his Cause, and assisted him to prosecute his Enemies, which he did, till he brought them all to Justice, expos'd them to the last Degree, obtain'd the reparation of all his Losses, and a publick Decree of the Judges of his Justification and future Repose.

Indeed when I saw the Proceedings against this poor Man run to a heighth so extravagant and monstrous, when I found Malice, Forgery, Subornation, Perjury, and a thousand unjustifiable Things which their own Sense, if they had any, might ha' been their Protection against, and which any Child in the Moon might ha' told them must one time or other come upon the Stage and expose them; I began to think these People were all in the Crolian Plot too.

For really such Proceedings as these were the greatest pieces of Service to the Crolians as could possibly be done; for as it generally proves in other Places as well as in the Moon, that Mischief unjustly contriv'd falls upon the Head of the Authors, and redounds to their treble Dishonour, so it was here; the barbarity and inhumane Treatment of this Man, made the sober and honest Part even of the Solanarians themselves blush for their Brethren, and own that the Punishment awarded on them was just.

Thus the Crolians got ground by the Folly and Madness of their Enemies, and the very Engines and Plots laid to injure them, serv'd to bring their Enemies on the Stage, and expose both them and their Cause.

But this was not all, by these incessant Attacks on them as a Party, they began to come to their Senses out of a 50 Year slumber, they found the Law on their side, and the Government Moderate and Just; they found they might oppose Violence with Law, and that when they did fly to the Refuge of Justice, they always had the better of their Enemy; flusht with this Success, it put them upon considering what Fools they had been all along to bear the Insolence of a few hot-headed Men, who contrary to the true Intent and Meaning of the Queen, or of the Government, had resolv'd their Destruction.

It put them upon revolving the State of their own Case, and comparing it with their Enemies; upon Examining on what foot they stood, and tho' Establish'd upon a firm Law, yet a violent Party pushing at the overthrow of that Establishment, and dissolving the legal Right they had to their Liberty and Religion; it put them upon duly weighing the nearness of their approaching Ruin and Destruction, and finding things run so hard against them, reflecting upon the Extremity of their Affairs, and how if they had not drawn in the High Church-Champions to damn the Projects of their own Party, by running at such desperate Extremes as all Men of any Temper must of course abhor, they had been undone; truly now they began to consider, and to consult with one another what was to be done.

Abundance of Projects were laid before them, some too Dangerous, some too Foolish to be put in practice;

at last they resolv'd to consult with my Philosopher.

He had been but scurvily treated by them in his Troubles, and so Universally abandon'd by the Crolians, that even the Solunarians themselves insulted them on that Head, and laugh'd at them for expecting any Body should venture for them again. - But he forgetting their unkindness, ask'd them what it was they desir'd of him?

They told him, they had heard that he had reported he could put the Crolians in a way to secure themselves from any possibility of being insulted again by the Solunarians, and yet not disturb the publick Tranquility, nor break the Laws; and they desir'd him, if he knew such a Secret, he would communicate it to them, and they would be sure to remember to forget him for it as long as he liv'd.

He frankly told them he had said so, and it was true, he could put them in a way to do all this if they would follow his Directions. What's that, says one of the most earnest Enquirers? - 'Tis included in one Word, says he, UNITE.

This most significant Word, deeply and solidly reflected upon, put them upon strange and various Conjectures, and many long Debates they had with themselves about it; at last they came again to him, and ask'd him what he mean't by it?

He told them he knew they were Strangers to the meaning of the thing, and therefore if they would meet him the next Day he would come prepar'd to explain himself; accordingly they meet, when instead of a long Speech they expected from him what sort of Union he mean't, and with who, he brings them a Thinking Press, or Cogitator, and setting it down, goes away without speaking one Word.

This Hyerogliphical Admonition was too plain not to let them all into his meaning; but still as they are an obstinate People, and not a little valuing themselves upon their own Knowledge and Penetration, they slighted the Engine and fell to off-hand-Surmises, Guesses and Supposes.

1. Some concluded he mean't Unite with the Solunarian Church, and they reflected upon his Understanding, that not being the Question in Hand, and something remote from their Intention, or the High Solunarians Desire.

2. Some mean't Unite to the moderate Party of the Solunarians, and this they said they had done already.

At last some being very Cunning, found it out, that it must be his meaning Unite one among another; and even there again they misunderstood him too; and some imagin'd he mean't down right Rebellion, Uniting Power, and Mobbing the whole Moon, but he soon convinc'd them of that too.

At last they took the Hint, that his Advice directed them to Unite their subdivided Parties into one general Interest, and to act in Concert upon one bottom, to lay aside the Selfish, Narrow, Suspicious Spirit; three Qualifications the Crolians were but too justly charg'd with, and begin to act with Courage, Unanimity and Largeness of Soul, to open their Eyes to their own Interest, maintain a regular and constant Correspondence with one another in all parts of the Kingdom, and to bring their civil Interest into a Form.

The Author of this Advice having thus brought them to understand, and approve his Proposal, they demanded his assistance for making the Essay, and 'tis a most wonderful thing to consider what a strange effect the alteration of their Measures had upon the whole Solunarian Nation.

As soon as ever they had settled the Methods they resolv'd to act in, they form'd a general Council of the Heads of their Party, to be always sitting, to reconcile Differences, to unite Parties, to suppress Feuds in their beginning.

They appointed 3 general Meetings in 3 of the most remote Parts of the Kingdom, to be half yearly, and one universal Meeting of Persons deputed to concert matters among them in General.

By that time these Meetings had sat but once, and the Conduct of the Council of 12 began to appear, 'twas a wonder to see the prodigious alteration it made all over the Country.

Immediately a Crolian would never buy any thing but of a Crolian; would hire no Servants, employ neither Porter nor Carman, but what were Crolians.

The Crolians in the Country that wrought and manag'd the Manufactures, would employ no body but Crolian Spinners, Crolian Weavers, and the like.

In their capital City the Merchandizing Crolians would freight no Ships but of which the Owners and Commanders were Crolians.

They call'd all their Cash out of the Solunarian Bank; and as the Act of the Cortez confirming the Bank then in being seem'd to be their Support, they made it plain that Cash and Credit will make a Bank without a publick Settlement of Law; and without these all the Laws in the Moon will never be able to support it.

They brought all their running Cash into one Bank, and settled a sub-Cash depending upon the Grand-Bank in every Province of the Kingdom; in which, by a strict Correspondence and crediting their Bills, they might be able to settle a Paper Credit over the whole Nation.

They went on to settle themselves in all sorts of Trade in open Companies, and sold off their Interests in the publick Stocks then in Trade.

If the Government wanted a Million of Mony upon any Emergency, they were ready to lend it as a Body, not by different Sums and private Hands blended together with their Enemies, but as will appear at large presently, it was only Crolian Mony, and pass'd as such.

Nor were the Consequences of this New Model less considerable than the Proposer expected, for the Crolians being generally of the Trading Manufacturing part of the World, and very Rich; the influence this method had upon the common People, upon Trade, and upon the Publick was very considerable every way.

1. All the Solunarian Trades-Men and Shop-keepers were at their Wits end, they sat in their Shops and had little or nothing to do, while the Shops of the Crolians were full of Customers, and their People over Head and Ears in Business; this turn'd many of the

Solunarian Trades-Men quite off of the hooks, and they began to break and decay strangely, till at last a great many of them to prevent their utter Ruin, turn'd Crolians on purpose to get a Trade; and what forwarded that part of it was, that when a Solunarian, who had little or no Trade before, came but over to the Crolians, immediately every Body come to Trade with him, and his Shop would be full of Customers, so that this presently encreas'd the number of the Crolians.

2. The poor People in the Countries, Carders, Spinners, Weavers, Knitters, and all sorts of Manufacturers, run in Crowds to the Crolian Temples for fear of being starv'd, for the Crolians were two thirds of the Masters or Employers in the Manufactures all over the Country, and the Poor would ha' been starv'd and undone if they had cast them out of Work. Thus infenfibly the Crolians encreas'd their number.

3. The Crolians being Men of vast Cash, they no sooner withdrew their Mony from the General Bank but the Bank languisht, Credit sunk, and in a short time they had little to do, but dissolv'd of Course.

One thing remain'd which People expected would ha' put a Check to this Undertaking, and that was a way of Trading in Classes, or Societies, much like our East-India Companies in England; and these depending upon publick Privileges granted by the Queen of the Country, or her Predecessors, no Body could Trade to those Parts but the Persons who had those priviledges: The cunning Crolians, who had great Stocks in those Trades, and foresaw they could not Trade by themselves without the publick Grant or Charter, contriv'd a way to get almost all that Capital Trade into their Hands as follows.

They concerted Matters, and all at once fell to selling off their Stock, giving out daily Reports that they would be no longer concern'd, that it was a losing Trade, that the Fund at bottom was good for nothing, and that of two Societies the Old one had not 20 per Cent. to divide, all their Debts being paid; that the New Society had Traded several Years, but if they were dissolv'd could not say that they had got any thing; and that this must be a Cheat at last, and so they resolv'd to sell.

By this Artifice, they daily offering to Sale, and yet in all their Discourse discouraging the thing they were to sell no Body could be found to buy.

The offering a thing to Sale and no Bidders, is a certain never-failing prospect of a lowring the Price; from this Method therefore the value of all the Banks, Companies, Societies and Stocks in the Country fell to be little or nothing worth; and that was to be bought for 40 or 45 Lunarians that was formerly sold at 150, and so in proportion of all the rest.

All this while the Crolians employ'd their Emissaries to buy up privately all the Interest or Shares in these Things that any of the Solunarian Party would sell.

This Plot took readily, for these Gentlemen exposing the weakness of these Societies, and running down the value of their Stocks, and at the same time warily buying at the lowest Prices, not only in time got Possession of the whole Trade, with their Grants, Privileges and Stocks, but got into them at a prodigiously low and despicable Price.

They had no sooner thus worm'd them out of the

Trade, and got the greatest part of the Effects in their own Hands, and consequently the whole Management, but they run up the Price of the Funds again as high as ever, and laught at the folly of those that sold out.

Nor could the other People make any Reflections upon the honesty of the practice, for it was no Original, but had its birth among the Solunarians themselves, of whom 3 or 4 had frequently made a Trade of raising and lowring the Funds of the Societies by all the Clandestine Contrivances in the World, and had ruin'd abundance of Families to raise their own Fortunes and Estates.

One of the greatest Merchants in the Moon rais'd himself by this Method to such a heighth of Wealth, that he left all his Children married to Grandees, Dukes, and Great Folks; and from a Mechanick Original, they are now rankt among the Lunarian Nobility, while multitudes of ruin'd Families helpt to build his Fortune, by sinking under the Knavery of his Contrivance.

His Brother in the same Iniquity, being at this time a Man of the Feather, has carry'd on the same intrieguing Trade with all the Face and Front imaginable; it has been nothing with him to persuade his most intimate Friends to Sell, or Buy, just as he had occasion for his own Interest to have it rise, or fall, and so to make his own Market of their Misfortune. Thus he has twice rais'd his Fortunes, for the House of Feathers demolisht him once, and yet he has by the same clandestine Management work'd himself up again.

This civil way of Robbing Houses, for I can esteem it no better, was carry'd on by a middle sort of People, call'd in the Moon BLOUTEGONDEGOURS, which which signifies Men with two Tongues, or in English, Stock-Jobbing Brokers.

These had formerly such an unlimited Power and were so numerous, that indeed they govern'd the whole Trade of the Country; no Man knew when he Bought or Sold, for tho' they pretended to Buy and Sell, and Manage for other Men whose Stocks they had very much at Command, yet nothing was more frequent than when they bought a thing cheap, to buy it for themselves; if dear, for their Employer; if they were to Sell, if the Price rise, it was Sold, if it Fell, it was Unsold; and by this Art no body got any Mony but themselves, that at last, excepting the two capital Men we spoke of before, these govern'd the Prizes of all things, and nothing could be Bought or Sold to Advantage but thro' their hands; and as the Profit was prodigious, their number encreas'd accordingly, so that Business seem'd engross'd by these Men, and they govern'd the main Articles of Trade.

This Success, and the Imprudence of their Conduct, brought great Complaints against them to the Government, and a Law was made to restrain them, both in Practice and Number.

This Law has in some measure had its Effect, the number is not only lessen'd, but by chance some honester Men than usual are got in among them, but they are so very, very, very Few, hardly enough to save a Man's Credit that shall vouch for them.

Nay, some People that pretend to understand their Business better than I do, having been of their Number, have affirm'd, it is impossible to be honest in the employment.

I confess when I began to search into the Conduct of these Men, at least of some of them, I found there were abundance of black Stories to be told of them, a great deal known, and a great deal more unknown; for they were from the beginning continually Encroaching into all sorts of People and Societies, and in Conjunction with some that were not qualify'd by Law, but meerly Voluntarily, call'd in the Moon by a hard long Word, in English signifying PROJECTORS these erected Stocks in Shadows, Societies in Nubibus, and Bought and Sold meer Vapour, Wind, Emptiness and Bluster for Mony, till they drew People in to lay out their Cash, and then laught at them.

Thus they erected Paper Societies, Linnen Societies, Sulphur Societies, Copper Societies, Glass Societies, Sham Banks, and a thousand mock Whimsies to hook unwary People in; at last sold themselves out, left the Bubble to float a little in the Air, and then vanish of it self.

The other sort of People go on after all this; and tho' these Projectors began to be out of Fashion, they always found one thing or other to amuse and deceive the Ignorant, and went Jobbing on into all manner of things, Publick as well as Private, whether the Revenue, the Publick Funds, Loans, Annuities, Bear-Skins, or any thing.

Nay they were once grown to that extravagant highth, that they began to Stock-Job the very Feathers of the Consolidator, and in time the King's employing those People might have had what Feathers they had occasion for, without concerning the Proprietors of the

Lands much about them.

'Tis true this began to be notorious, and receiv'd some check in a former meeting of the Feathers; but even now, when I came away, the three Years expiring, and by Course a new Consolidator being to be built, they were as busie as ever. Bidding, Offering, Procuring, Buying, Selling, and Jobbing of Feathers to who bid most; and notwithstanding several late wholesome and strict Laws against all manner of Collusion, Bribery and clandestine Methods, in the Countries procuring these Feathers; never was the Moon in such an uproar about picking and culling the Feathers, such Bribery, such Drunkenness, such Caballing, especially among the High Solunarian Clergy and the Lazognians, such Feasting, Fighting and Distraction, as the like has never been known.

And that which is very Remarkable, all this not only before the Old Consolidator was broke up, but even while it was actually whole and in use.

Had this hurry been to send up good Feathers, there had been the less to say, but that which made it very strange to me was, that where the very worst of all the Feathers were to be found, there was the most of this wicked Work; and tho' it was bad enough every where, yet the greatest bustle and contrivance was in order to send up the worst Feathers they could get.

And indeed some Places such Sorry, Scoundrel, Empty, Husky, Wither'd, Decay'd Feathers were offer'd to the Proprietors, that I have sometimes wonder'd any one could have the Impudence to send up such ridiculous Feathers to make a Consolidator, which, as is before observ'd, is an Engine of such Beauty,

Usefulness and Necessity.

And still in all my Observation, this Note came in my way, there was always the most bustle and disturbance about the worst Feathers.

It was really a melancholly Thing to consider, and had this Lunar World been my Native Country, I should ha' been full of concern to see that one thing, on which the welfare of the whole Nation so much depended, put in so ill a Method, and gotten into the management of such Men, who for Mony would certainly ha' set up such Feathers, that wherever the Consolidator should be form'd, it would certainly over-set the first Voyage; and if the whole Nation should happen to be Embarkt in it, on the dangerous Voyage to the Moon, the fall would certainly give them such a Shock, as would put them all into Confusion, and open the Door to the Gallunarian, or any Foreign Enemy to destroy them.

It was really strange that this should be the Case, after so many Laws, and so lately made, against it; but in this, those People are too like our People in England, who have the best Laws the worst executed of any Nation under Heaven.

For in the Moon this hurry about choosing of Feathers was grown to the greatest heighth imaginable, as if it encreast by the very Laws that were made to suppress it; for now at a certain publick Place where the Bloutegondegours us'd to meet every Day, any Body that had but Mony enough might buy a Feather at a reasonable Rate, and never go down into the Country to fetch it; nay, the Trade grew so hot, that of a sudden as if no other Business was in Hand, all people were upon it , and the whole Market was chang'd from

Selling of Bear-Skins, to Buying of Feathers.

Some gave this for a Reason why all the Stocks of the Societies fell so fast, but there were other Reasons to be given for that, such as Clubs, Cabals, Stock-Jobbers, Knights, Merchants and Thie - s. I mean a private Sort, not such as are frequently Hang'd there, but of a worse Sort, by how much they merit that Punishment more, but are out of the reach of the Law, can Rob and pick Pockets in the Face of the Sun, and laugh at the Families they Ruin, bidding Defiance to all legal Resentment.

To this height things were come under the growing Evil of this sort of People.

And yet in the very Moon where, as I have noted, the People are so exceeding clear Sighted, and have such vast helps to their perceptive Faculties, such Mists are sometimes cast before the publick Understanding, that they cannot see the general Interest.

This was manifest, in that just as I came away from that Country, the great Council of their Wise Men, the Men of the Feather, were a going to repeal the old Law of Restraining the Number of these People; and tho' as it was, there was not Employment for half of them, there being 100 in all, and not above 5 honest ones; yet when I came away they were going to encrease their Number. I have nothing to say to this here, only that all Wise Men that understand Trade were very much concern'd at it, and lookt upon it as a most destructive Thing to the Publick, and forboding the same mischiefs that Trade suffer'd before.

It was the particular Misfortune to these Lunar People

that this Country had a better Stock of Governors in all Articles of their Well-fare, than in their Trade; their Law Affairs had good Judges, their Church good Patriarchs, except, as might be excepted; their State good Ministers, their Army good Generals, and their Consolidator good Feathers; but in Matters relating to Trade, they had this particular Misfortune, that those Cases always came before People that did not understand them.

Even the Judges themselves were often found at a Loss to determine Causes of Negoce, such as Protests, Charter-Parties, Avarages, Baratry, Demorage of Ships, Right of detaining Vessels on Demorage, and the like; nay, the very Laws themselves are fain to be silent and yield in many things a Superiority to the Custom of Merchants.

And here I began to Congratulate my Native Country, where the Prudence of the Government has provided for these things, by Establishing in a Commission of Trade some of the most experienc'd Gentlemen in the Nation, to Regulate, Settle, Improve, and revive Trade in General, by their unwearyed Labours, and most consummate Understanding; and this made me pity these Countries, and think it would be an Action worthy of this Nation, and be spoken of for Ages to come to their Glory, if in meer Charity they would appoint or depute these Gentlemen to go a Voyage to those Countries of the Moon, and bless those Regions with the Schemes of their sublime Undertakings, and discoveries in Trade.

But when I was expressing my self thus, my Philosopher interrupted me, and told me I should see they were already furnisht for that purpose, when I came to examine the publick Libraries, of which by it self.

But I was farther confirm'd in my Observation of the weakness of the publick Heads of that Country, as to Trade, when I saw another most preposterous Law going forward among them, the Title of which was specious, and contain'd something relating to employing the Poor, but the substance of it absolutely destructive to the very Nature of their Trade, tending to Transposing, Confounding and Destroying their Manufactures, and to the Ruin of all their Home-Commerce; never was Nation so blind to their own Interest as these Lunarian Law Makers, and the People who were the Contrivers of this Law were so vainly Conceited, so fond of the guilded Title, and so positively Dogmatick, that they would not hear the frequent Applications of Persons better acquainted with those things than themselves, but pusht it on meerly by the strength of their Party, for the Vanity of being Authors of such a Contrivance.

But to return to the new Model of the Crolians. The advice of the Lunarian Philosopher run now thro' all their Affairs, UNITE was the Word thro' all the Nation, in Trade, in Cash, in Stocks, as I noted before.

If a Solunarian Ship was bound to any Out Port, no Crolian would load any Goods aboard; if any Ship came to seek Freight abroad, none of the Crolians Correspondents would Ship any thing unless they knew the Owners were Crolians; the Crolian Merchants turn'd out all their Solunarian Masters, Sailors and Captains from their Ships; and thus, as the Solunarians would have them be separated in respect of the Government, Profits, Honours and Offices, they resolv'd to separate in every thing else too, and to stand by themselves.

At last, upon some publick Occasion, the publick Treasurers of the Land sent to the capital City, to borrow 500000 Lunarians upon very good Security of establisht Funds; truly no Body would lend any Mony, or at least they could not raise above a 5th part of that Sum, enquiring at the Bank, at their general Societies Cash, and other Places, all was languid and dull, and no Mony to be had; but being inform'd that the Crolians had erected a Bank of their own, they sent thither, and were answered readily, that whatever Sum the Government wanted, was at their Service, only it was to be lent not by particular Persons, but such a Grandee being one of the prime Nobility, and who the Crolians now call'd their Protector, was to be Treated with about it.

The Government saw no harm in all this; here was no Law broken, here was nothing but Oppression answered with Policy, and Mischief fenc'd against with Reason.

The Government therefore took no Notice of it, nor made any Scruple when they wanted any Mony to Treat with this Nobleman, and borrow any Sum of the Crolians, as Crolians; on the contrary in the Name of the Crolians; their Head or Protector presented their Addresses and Petitions, procur'd Favours on one Hand, and Assistance on the other; and thus by degrees and insensibly the Crolians became a Politick Body, settled and establish'd by Orders and Rules among themselves; and while a Spirit of Unanimity thus run thro' all their Proceedings, their Enemies could never hurt them, their Princes always saw it was their Interest to keep Measures with them, and they were sure to have Justice upon any Complaint whatsoever.

When I saw this, it forc'd me to reflect upon Affairs in our own Country; Well, said I, 'tis happy for England that our Dissenters have not this Spirit of Union and Largeness of Heart among them; for if they were not a Narrow, mean-Spirited, short-Sighted, self-Preserving, friend-Betraying, poor-Neglecting People, they might ha' been every way as Safe, as Considerable, as Regarded and as Numerous as the Crolians in the Moon; but it is not in their Souls to do themselves Good, nor to Espouse, or Stand by those that would do it for them; and 'tis well for the Church-Men that it is so, for many Attempts have been made to save them, but their own narrowness of Soul, and dividedness in Interest has always prevented its being effectual, and discourag'd all the Instruments that ever attempted to serve them.

'Tis confest the Case was thus at first among the Crolians, they were full of Divisions among themselves, as I have noted already of the Solunarians, and the unhappy Feuds among them, had always not only expos'd them to the Censure, Reproach and Banter of their Solunarian Enemies, but it had serv'd to keep them under, prevent their being valued in the Government, and given the other Party vast Advantages against.

But the Solunarians driving thus furiously at their Destruction and entire Ruin, open'd their Eyes to the following Measures for their preservation: And here again the high Solunarians may see, and doubtless whenever they made use of the Lunar-Glasses they must see it, that nothing could ha' driven the Crolians to make use of such Methods for their Defence, but the rash Proceedings of their own warm Men, in order to suppressing the whole Crolian Interest. And this might inform our Country-men of the Church of England, that it cannot but be their Interest to Treat their Brethren with Moderation and Temper, least their Extravagances should one time or other drive the other as it were by Force into their Senses, and open their Eyes to do only all those Things which by Law they may do, and which they are laught at by all the World for not doing.

This was the very Case in the Moon: The Philosopher, or pretended-such as before, had often publish'd, that it was their Interest to UNITE; but their Eyes not being open to the true Causes and Necessity of it, their Ears were shut against the Council, till Oppression and Necessities drove them to it.

Accordingly they entred into a serious Debate, of the State of their own Affairs, and finding the Advice given, very reasonable; they set about it, and the Author gave them a Model, Entitl'd An enquiry into what the Crolians may lawfully do, to prevent the certain Ruin of their Interest, and bring their Enemies to Peace.

I will not pretend to examine the Contents of this sublime Tract; but from this very Day, we found the Crolians in the Moon, acting quite on a different Foot from all their former Conduct, putting on a new Temper, and a new Face, as you have hear'd.

All this while the hot Solunarians cried out Plots, Associations, Confederacies, and Rebellions, when indeed here was nothing done but what the Laws justify'd, what Reason directed, and what had the Crolians but made use of the Cogitator, they would ha' done 40 Year before.

The Truth is, the other People had no Remedy, but to cry Murther, and make a Noise; for the Crolians went on with their Affairs, and Establisht themselves so, that when I came away, they were become a most Solid, and well United Body, made a considerable Figure in the Nation, and yet the Government was easy; for the Solunarians found when they had attain'd the utmost end of their Wishes, her Solunarian Majesty was as safe as before, and the Crolians Property being secur'd, they were as Loyal Subjects as the Solunarians, as consistent with Monarchy, as useful to it, and as pleas'd with it.

I cannot but Remark here, that this Union of the Crolians among themselves had another Consequence, which made it appear it was not only to their own Advantage, but to the general Good of all the Natien.

For, by little, and little, the Feuds of the Parties cool'd, and the Solunarians began to be better reconcil'd to them; the Government was easy and safe, and the private Quarrels, as I have been told since, begin to be quite forgot.

What Blindness, said I to my self, has possest the Dissenters in our unhappy Country of England, where by eternal Discords, Feuds, Distrusts and Disgusts among themselves, they always fill their Enemies with Hopes, that by pushing at them, they may one time or other compleat their Ruin; which Expectation has always serv'd as a means to keep open the Quarrel; whereas had the Dissenters been United in Interest,

Affection and Mannagement among themselves, all this Heat had long ago been over, and the Nation, tho' there had been two Opinions had retain'd but one Interest, been joyn'd in Affection, and Peace at Home been rais'd up to that Degree that all Wise Men wish, as it is now among the Inhabitants of the World in the Moon.

Tis true, in all the Observations I made in this Lunar Country, the vast deference paid to the Persons of Princes began to lessen, and whatever Respect they had for the Office, they found it necessary frequently to tell the World that on occasion, they could Treat them with less Respect than they pretended to owe them.

For about this time, the Divine Right of Kings, and the Inheritances of Princes in the Moon, met with a terrible Shock, and that by the Solunarian Party themselves; and insomuch that even my Philosopher, and he was none of the Jure Divino Men, neither declar'd, against it.

They made Crowns perfect Foot-balls, set up what Kings they would, and pull'd down such as they did not like, Ratitione Voluntas, right or wrong, as they thought best, of which some Examples shall be given by and by.

After I had thus enquir'd into the Historical Affairs of this Lunar Nation, which for its Similitude to my Native Country, I could not but be inquisitive in; I wav'd a great many material Things, which at least I cannot enter upon the Relation of here, and began to enquire into their Affairs abroad.

I think I took notice in the beginning of my Account of these parts, that I found them engag'd in a tedious and bloody War, with one of the most mighty Monarchs of all the Moon.

I must therefore hint, that among the multitude of things, which for brevity sake I omit, the Reader may observe these were some.

1. That this was the same Monarch who harbour'd and entertain'd the Abrogratzian Prince, who was fled as before, and who we are to call the King of Gallunaria.

2. I have omitted the Account of a long and bloody War, which lasted a great many Years, and which the present Queens Predecessor, mannag'd with a great deal of Bravery and Conduct, and finisht very much to his own Glory, and the Nations Advantage.

3. I have too much omitted to Note, how Barbarously the High Solunarian Church Men treated him for all his Services, upbraided him with the Expence of the War; and tho' he sav'd them all from Ruin and Abrogratzianism, yet had not one good Word for him, and indeed 'tis with some difficulty that I pass this over, because it might be necessary to observe, besides what is said before, that Ingratitude is a Vice in Nature, and practis'd every where, as well as in England. So that we need not upbraid the Party among us with their ill Treatment of the late King, for these People us'd their good King every Jot as bad, till their unkindness perfectly broke his Heart.

Here also I am oblig'd to omit the Historical Part of the War, and of the Peace that follow'd; only I must observe that this Peace was very Precarious, Short and

Unhappy, and in a few Months the War broke out again, with as much Fury as ever.

In this War happen'd one of the strangest, unaccountable and most preposterous Actions, that ever a People in their National Capacity could be guilty of.

Certainly if our People in England, who pretend that Kingship is Jure Divino, did but know the Story of which I speak, they would be quite of another Mind; wherefore I crave leave to relate part of the History, or Original of this last War, as a necessary Introduction to the proper Observations I shall make upon it.

There was a King of a certain Country in the Moon, call'd in their Language, Ebronia, who was formerly a Confederate with the Solunarians. This Prince dying without Issue, the great Monarch we speak of, seiz'd upon all his Dominions as his Right. - Tho' if I remember right, he had formerly Sworn never to lay Claim to it, and after that by a subsequent Treaty had agreed with the Solunarian Prince, that another Monarch who claim'd a Right as well as he, should divide it between them.

The breach of this Agreement, and seizing this Kingdom, put almost all the Lunar World into a Flame, and War hung over the Heads of all the Northern Nations of the Moon, for several Claims were made to the Succession by other Princes, and particularly by a certain Potent Prince call'd the Eagle, of an Ancient Family, whose Lunar Name I cannot well express, but in English it signifies the Men of the great Lip; whether it was Originally a sort of a Nick Name, or whether they had any such thing as a great Lip Hereditary to the Family, by which they were distinguisht, is not worth my while to Examine.

'Tis without question that the successive Right, if their Lunar Successions, are Govern'd as ours are in this world, devolv'd upon this Man with the Lip and his Families; but the Gallunarian Monarch brought things so to pass, by his extraordinary Conduct, that the Ebronian King was drawn in by some of his Nobility, who this Prince had Bought and Brib'd to betray their Country to his Interest, and particularly a certain High Priest of that Country, to make an Assignment, or deed of Gift of all his Dominions to the Grandson of this Gallunarian Monarch.

By Vertue of this Gift, or Legacy, as soon as the King dyed, who was then languishing, and as the other Parry alledg'd, not in a very good capacity to make a Will; the Gallunarian King sent his Grandson to seize upon the Crown, and backing him with suitable Forces, took Possession of all his strong Fortifications and Frontiers.

Nor was this all, the Man with the Lip indeed talkt big, and threatned War immediately, but the Solunarians were so unsettl'd at Home, so unprepar'd for War, having but just dismist their Auxiliar Troops, and disbanded their own, and the Prince was so ill serv'd by his Subjects, that both he and a Powerful Neighbour, Nations in the same Interest, were meerly Bullyed by this Gallunarian; and as he threatned immediately to Invade them, which they were then in no Condition to prevent, he forc'd them both to submit to his Demand, tacitely allow what he had done in breaking the Treaty with him, and at last openly acknowledge his new King.

This was indeed a most unaccountable Step, but there was a necessity to plead, for he was at their very Doors with his Forces; and this Neighbouring People, who they call Mogenites, could not resist him without help from the Solunarians, which they were very backward in, notwithstanding the earnest Sollicitations of their Prince, and notwithstanding they were oblig'd to do it by a solemn Treaty.

These delays oblig'd them to this strange Step of acknowledging the Invasion of their Enemy, and pulling off the Hat to the New King he had set up.

'Tis true, the Policy of these Lunar Nations was very Remarkable in this Case, and they out-witted the Gallunarian Monarch in it; for by the owning this Prince, whom they immediately after Declar'd a Usurper, and made War against; they stopt the Mouth of the Gallunarian his Grandfather, took from him all pretence of Invading them, and making him believe they were Sincere, Wheedl'd him to restore several Thousands of their Men who he had taken Prisoners in the Frontier Towns of the Ebronians.

Had the Gallunarian Prince had but the forecast to ha' seen, that this was but a forc'd pretence to gain Time, and that as soon as they had their Troops clear and Time to raise more, they would certainly turn upon him again, he would never ha' been put by with so weak a Trifle as the Ceremony of Congratulation; whereas had he immediately pusht at them with all his Forces, they must ha' been Ruin'd, and he had carry'd his Point without much Interruption.

But here he lost his Opportunity, which he never retriev'd; for 'tis in the Moon, just as 'tis here, when an

Occasion is lost, it is not easy to be recover'd, for both the Solunarians and the Mogenites quickly threw off the Mask, and declaring this new Prince an Usurper, and his Grandfather an Unjust breaker of Treaties, they prepar'd for War against them both.

As to the Honesty of this matter, my Philosopher and I differ'd extremely, he exclaim'd against the Honour of acknowledging a King, with a design to Depose him, and pretending Peace when War is design'd; tho' 'tis true, they are too customary in our World; but however, as to him I insisted upon the lawfulness of it, from the universal Custom of Nations, who generally do things ten times more Preposterous and Inconsistent, when they suit their Occasions. Yet I hope no Body will think I am recommending them by this Relation to the Practice of our own Nations, but rather exposing them as unaccountable things never to be put in Practice, without quitting all pretences to Justice and national Honesty.

The Case was this.

As upon the Progress of Matters before related, the Solunarians and Mogenites had made a formal acknowledgment of this new Monarch, the Grandson of the Gallunarian King, so as I have hinted already, they had no other design than to Depose him, and pull him down.

Accordingly, as soon as by the aforesaid Wile they had gain'd Breath, and furnisht themselves with Forces, they declar'd War against both the Gallunarian King, and his Grandson, and entred into strict Confederacy with the Man of the great Lip, who was the Monarch of the Eagle, and who by right of Succession, had the true Claim to the Ebronian Crowns.

In these Declarations they alledge that Crowns do not descend by Gift, nor are Kingdoms given away by Legacy, like a Gold Ring at a Funeral, and therefore this young Prince could have no Right, the former deceas'd King having no Right to dispose it by Gift.

I must allow, that judging by our Reason, and the Practice in our Countries here, on this side the Moon; this seem'd plain, and I saw no difference in matters of Truth there, or here, but Right and Liberty both of Princes and People seems to be the same in that World, as it is in this, and upon this account I thought the Reasons of this War very Just, and that the Claim of Right to the Succession of the Ebronian Crown, was undoubtedly in the Man with the Lip, and his Heirs, and so far the War was most Just, and the Design reasonable.

And thus far my Lunar Companion agreed with me, and had they gone on so, says he, they had my good Wishes, and my Judgment had been Witness to my Pretences, that they were in the right.

But in the prosecution of this War, says he, they went on to one of the most Impolitick, Ridiculous, Dishonest, and Inconsistent Actions, that ever any Nation in the Moon was guilty of; the Fact was thus.

Having agreed among themselves that the Ebronian Crown should not be possest by the Gallunarian King's Grandson, they in the next Place began to consider who should have it.

The Man with the Lip had the Title, but he had a great

Government of his own, Powerful, Happy and Remote, being as is noted, the Lord of the great Eagle, and he told them he could not pretend to come to Ebronia to be a King there; his eldest Son truly was not only declar'd Heir apparent to his Father, but had another Lunarian Kingdom of his own still more remote than that, and he would not quit all this for the Crown of Ebronia, so it was concerted by all the Confederated Parties, that the second Son of this Prince, the Man with the Lip, should be declar'd King, and here lay the Injustice of all the Case.

I confess at my first examining this Matter, I did not see far into it, nor could I reach the Dishonesty of it, and perhaps the Reader of these Sheets may be in the same Case; but my old Lunarian Friend being continually exclaiming against the Matter, and blaming his Country-men the Solunarians for the Dishonesty of it, but especially the Mogenites, he began to be something peevish with me that I should be so dull as not to reach it, and askt me if he should screw me into the Thinking-Press for the Clearing up my Understanding.

At last he told me he would write his particular Sentiments of this whole Affair in a Letter to me, which he would so order as it should effectually open mine Eyes; which indeed it did, and so I believe it will the Eyes of all that read it; to which purpose I have obtain'd of the Author to assist me in the Translation of it, he having some Knowledge also in our Sublunar Languages.

The Sustance of a Letter, wrote to the Author of these Sheets, while he was in the Regions of the Moon.

'Friend from the Moon,

'According to my promise, I hereby give you a Scheme of Solunarian Honesty, join'd with Mogenite Policy, and my Opinion of the Action of my Country-men and their Confederates, in declaring their new made Ebronian King.

'The Mogenites and Solunarians are look'd upon here to be the Original Contrivers of this ridiculous piece of Pageantry, and tho' some of their Neighbours are suppos'd to have a Hand in it, yet we all lay it at the door of their Politicks, and for the Honesty of it let them answer it if they can.

''Tis observ'd here, that as soon as the King of Gallunaria had declar'd that he accepted the Will and Disposition of the Crown of Ebronia, in favour of his Grandson, and that according to the said Disposition, he had own'd him for King; and in order to make it effectual, had put him into immediate Possession of the Kingdom. The Mogenites and their Confederates made wonderful Clamours at the Injustice of his Proceedings, and particularly on account of his breaking the Treaty then lately entred into with the King of the Solunarians and the Mogenites, for the settling the Matter of Right and Possession, in case of the Demise of the Ebronian King.

'However, the King of Gallunaria had no sooner plac'd his Grandson on the Throne, but the Mogenites and other Nations, and to all our Wonder, the King of Solunaria himself acknowledg'd him, own'd him, sent their Ministers, and Compliments of Congratulation, and the like, giving him the Title of King of Ebronia.

'Tho' this proceeding had something of Surprize in it, and all Men expected to see something more than ordinary Politick in the effect of it, yet it did not give half the astonishment to the Lunar World, as this unaccountable Monster of Politicks begins to do.

'We have here two unlucky Fellows, call'd Pasquin and Marforio, these had a long Dialogue about this very Matter, and Pasquin as he always lov'd Mischief, told a very unlucky Story to his Comrade, of a high Mogenite Skipper, as follows.

'A Mogenite Ship coming from a far Country, the Custom House Officers found some Goods on Board, which were Controband, and for which they pretended the Ship and Goods were all Confiscated; the Skipper, or Captain in a great Fright, comes up to the Custom-House, and being told he must Swear to something relating to his taking in those Goods, reply'd in his Country Jargon, Ya, dat sall Ick doen Myn Heer; or in English, Ay, Ay, I'll Swear. - But finding they did not assure him that it would clear his Ship he scruples the Oath again, at which they told him it would clear his Ship immediately. Hael, well Myn Heer, says the Mogen Man, vat mot Ick sagen, Ick sall all Swear myn Skip to salvare, i.e. I shall Swear any thing to save my Skip.

'We apply this Story thus.

'If the Mogenites did acknowledge the King of Ebronia, we did believe it was done to save the Skip; and when they reproacht the Gallunarian King, with breaking the Treaty of Division, we us'd to say we would all break thro' twice as many Engagements for half as much Advantage.

'This setting up a new King, against a King on the Throne, Acknowledg'd and Congratulated by them, is not only look'd on in the Lunar World, as a thing Ridiculous, but particularly Infamous, that they should first acknowledge a King, and then set up the Title of another. If the Title of the first Ebronian King be good, this must be an Impostor, an Usurper of another Man's Right; if it was not good, why did they acknowledge him, and give him the full Title of all the Ebronian Dominions? Caress and Congratulate him, and make a publick Action of it to his Ambassador.

'Will they tell us they were Bully'd, and Frighted into it? that is to own they may be hufft into an ill Action; for owing a Man in the Posession of what is none of his own, is an ill thing, and he that may be hufft into one ill Action, may by Consequence be hufft into another, and so into any thing.

'What will they say for doing it? we have heard there has been in the World you came from, a way found out to own Kings de Facto, but not de Jure; if they will fly to that ridiculous Shift, let them tell the World so, that we may know what they mean, for those foolish things are not known here.

'If they own'd the King of Ebronia voluntarily, and acknowledg'd his Right as we thought they had; how then can this young Gentleman have a Title, unless they have found out a new Division, and so will have two Kings of Ebronia, make them Partners, and have a Gallunarian King of Ebronia, and a Mogenite King of Ebronia, both together?

'Our Lunar Nations, Princes and States, whatever they may do in your World, always seek for some Pretences at least to make their Actions seem Honest, whither they are so or no; and therefore they generally publish Memorials, Manifesto's and Declarations, of their Reasons why, and on what account they do so, or so; that those who have any Grounds to charge them with Unjustice, may be answer'd, and silenc'd; 'tis for the People in your Country, to fall upon their Neighbours, only because they will do it, and make probability of Conquest, a sufficient Reason of Conquest; the Lunarian Nations are seldom so destitute of Modesty, but that they will make a shew of Justice, and make out the Reasons of their Proceedings; and tho' sometimes we find even the Reasons given for some Actions are weak enough; yet it is a bad Cause indeed, that can neither have a true Reason, nor a pretended one. The custom of the Moon has oblig'd us to show so much respect to Honesty, that when our Actions have the least colour of Honesty, yet we will make Reasons to look like a Defence, whether it be so or no.

'But here is an Action that has neither reality, nor pretence, here is not Face enough upon it to bear an Apology. First, they acknowledge one King, and then set up another King against him; either they first acknowledg'd a wrong King, and thereby became Parties to a Usurper, or they act now against all the Rules of common Justice in the World, to set up a sham King, to pull down a true one, only because 'tis their Interest to have it so.

'This makes the very Name of a Solunarian scandalous to all the Moon, and Mankind look upon them with the utmost Prejudice, as if they were a Nation who had sold all their Honesty to their Interest; and who could act this way to Day, and that way to Morrow, without any regard to Truth, or the Rule of Honour, Equity or

Conscience; This is Swearing any thing to save the Skip; and never let any Man Reproach the Gallunarian King with breaking the Treaty of Division, and disregarding the Faith and Stipulations of Leagues; for this is an Action so inconsistent with it self, so incongruous to common Justice, to the Reason and Nature of things, that no History of any of these latter Times can parallel it, and 'tis past the Power of Art to make any reasonable Defence for it.

'Indeed some lame Reasons are given for it by our Polititians. First, they say the Prince with the great Lip was extremely prest by the Gallunarians at Home in his own Country, and not without apprehensions of seeing them e'er long, under the Walls of his capital City.

'From this circumstance of the Man with the Lip, 'twas not irrational to expect that he might be induc'd to make a separate Peace with the Gallunarians, and serve them as he did once the Prince of Berlindia at the Treaty of Peace in a former War, where he deserted him after the solemnest Engagements never to make Peace without him; but his pressing Occasions requiring it, concluded a Peace without him, and left him to come out of the War, as well as he could, tho' he had come into it only for his Assistance. Now finding him in danger of being ruin'd by the Gallunarian Power, and judging from former Practice in like Cases, that he might be hurry'd into a Peace, and leave them in the Lurch; they have drawn him into this Labrinth, as into a Step, which can never be receded from without the utmost Affront and Disgrace, either to the Family of the Gallunarian, or of the Lip; an Action which in its own Nature, is a Defiance of the whole Gallunarian Power, and without any other Manifesto, may be taken as a Declaration from the

House of the Lip, to the Gallunarian, that this War shall never end, till one of those two Families are ruin'd and reduc'd.

'What Condition the Prince with the Lip's Power is in, to make such a huff at this Time, shall come under Examination by and by; in the mean time the Solunarians have clench'd the Nail, and secur'd the War to last as long as they think convenient.

'If the Gallunarians should get the better, and reduce the Man with the Lip to Terms never so disadvantageous, he cannot now make a Peace without leave from the Solunarians and the Mogenites, least his Son should be ruin'd also. - Or if he should make Articles for himself, it must be with ten times the Dishonour that he might have done before.

'Politicians say, 'tis never good for a Prince to put himself into a case of Desperation. This is drawing the Sword, and throwing away the Scabbard; if a Disaster should befal him, his Retreat is impossible, and this must have been done only to secure the Man with the Lip from being hufft, or frighted into a separate Peace.

'The second Reason People here give, why the Solunarians are concerning themselves in this Matter, is drawn from Trade.

'The continuing of Ebronia in the Hands of the Gallunarians, will most certainly be the Destruction of the Solunarian and Mogenites Trade, both to that Kingdom, and the whole Seas on that side of the Moon; as this Article includes a fifth Part of all the Trade of the Moon, and would in Conjunction with the Gallunarians at last bring the Mastership of the Sea, out of the Hands of the other, so it would in effect be more detriment to those two Nations, than ten Kingdoms lost, if they had them to part with.

'This the Solunarians foreseeing, and being extremely sensible of the entire Ruin of their Trade, have left no Stone unturn'd to bring this piece of Pageantry on the Stage, by which they have hook'd in the Old Black Eagle to plunge himself over Head and Ears in the Quarrel, in such a manner, as he can never go back with any tolerable Honour; he can never quit his Son and the Crown of Ebronia, without the greatest Reproach and Disgrace of all the World in the Moon.

'Now whether one, or both of these Reasons are true in this Case, as most believe both of them to be true; the Policy of my Country-men, the Solunarians is visible indeed, but as for their Honesty, it is past finding out.

'But it is objected here, this Son of the Lip has an undoubted Right to the Crown of Ebronia. We do not Fight now to set up an Usurper, but to pull down an Usurper, and it has been made plain by the Manifesto, that the giving a Kingdom by Will, is no conveyance of Right; the Prince of the Eagle has an undoubted Right, and they Fight to maintain it.

'If this be true, then we must ask these High and Mighty Gentlemen how came they to recognize and acknowledge the present King on the Throne? why did they own an Usurper if he be such? either one or other must be an act of Cowardize and Injustice, and all the Politicks of the Moon cannot clear them of one of these two Charges; either they were Cowardly Knaves before, or else they must be Cunning Knaves now.

'If the Young Eagle has an undoubted Title now, so he had before, and they knew it as well before, as they do now; what can they say for themselves, why they should own a King, who they knew had no Title, or what can they say for going to pull down one that has a Title?

'I must be allow'd to distinguish between Fighting with a Nation, and Fighting with the King. For Example. Our Quarrel with the Gallunarians is with the whole Nation, as they are grown too strong for their Neighbours. But our Quarrel with Ebronia is not with the Nation, but with their King, and this Quarrel seems to be unjust in this particular, at least in them who own'd him to be King, for that put an end to the Controversy.

''Tis true, the Justice of publick Actions, either in Princes, or in States, is no such nice Thing, that any Body should be surpriz'd, to see the Government forfeit their Faith, and it seems the Solunarians are no more careful this way, than their Neighbours. But then those People should in especial manner forbear to reproach Other Nations and Princes, with the breaches which they themselves are subject too.

'As to the Eagle, we have nothing to say to the Honesty of his declaring his Son King of Ebronia, for as is hinted before, he never acknowledg'd the Title of the Usurper, but always declar'd, and insisted on his own undoubted Right, and that he would recover it if he could.

'Without doubt the Eagle has a Title by Proximity of Blood, founded on the renunciation of the King of Gallunaria formerly mention'd, and if the Will of the late King be Invalid, or he had no Right to give the Soveraignty of his Kingdoms away, then the Eagle is next Heir.

'But as we quit his Morals, and justify the Honesty of his Proceedings in the War, against the present King of Ebronia, so in this Action of declaring his second Son. We must begin to question his Understanding, and saying a respect of decency, it looks as if his Musical Head was out of Tune, to Illus tratellus. I crave leave to tell you a Story out of your own Country, which we have heard of hither. A French Man that could speak but broken English, was at the Court of England, when on some occasion he happen'd to hear the Title of the King of England read thus, Charles the II. King of England, Scotland France and Ireland.

'Vat is dat you say? says Monsieur, being a little affronted, the Man reads it again, as before. Charles the Second, King of England, Scotland, France and Ireland. - Charles the Second, King of France! Ma Foy, says the French Man, you can no read, Charles the Second, King of France, ha! ha! ha! Charles the Second, King of France, when he can catch. Any one may apply the Story, whether it was a true one or no.

'All the Lunar World looks on it, therefore, as a most Ridiculous, Senseless Thing, to make a Man a King of a Country he has not one Foot of Land in, nor can have a Foot there, but what he must Fight for. As to the probability of gaining it, I have nothing to say to it, but if we may guess at his Success there, by what has been done in other Parts of the Moon, we find he has Fought three Campaigns, to lose every Foot he had got.

'It had been much more to the Honour of the Eagle's

Conduct, and of the young Hero himself, first to ha' let him ha' fac'd his Enemy in the Field, and as soon as he had beaten him, the Ebronians would have acknowledg'd him fast enough; or his own Victorious Troops might have Proclaim'd him at the Gate of their Capital City; and if after all, the Success of the War had deny'd him the Crown he had fought for, he had the Honour to have shown his Bravery, and he had been where he was, a Prince of the Great Lip. A Son of the Eagle is a Title much more Honourable than a King Without a Crown, without Subjects, without a Kingdom, and another Man upon his Throne; but by this declaring him King, the old Eagle has put him under a necessity of gaining the Kingdom of Ebronia, which at best is a great hazard, or if he fails to be miserably despicable, and to bear all his Life the constant Chagrin of a great Title and no Possession.

'How ridiculous will this poor Young Gentleman look, if at last he should be forc'd to come Home again without his Kingdom? what a King of Clouts will he pass for, and what will this King-making old Gentlemen, his Father say, when the young Hero shall tell him, your Majesty has made me Mock King for all the World to laugh at.

"Twas certainly the weakest Thing that could be, for the Eagle thus to make him a King of that, which, were the probability greater than it is, he may easily, without the help of a Miracle, be disappointed of.

"Tis true, the Confederates talk big, and have lately had a great Victory, and if Talk will beat the King of Ebronia out of his Kingdom, he is certainly undone, but we do not find the Gallunarians part with any thing they can keep, nor that they quit any thing without

Blows; It must cost a great deal of Blood and Treasure before this War can be ended; if absolute Conquest on one side must be the Matter, and if the Design on Ebronia should miscarry, as one Voyage thither has done already, where are we then? Let any Man but look back, and consider what a sorry Figure your Confederate Fleet in your World had made, after their Andalusian Expedition, if they had not more by Fate than Conduct, chopt upon a Booty at Vigo as they came back.

'In the like condition, will this new King come back, if he should go for a Kingdom and should not Catch, as the French Man call'd it. 'Tis in the Sense of the probability of this miscarriage, that most Men wonder at these unaccountable Measures, and think the Eagles Councils look a little Wildish, as if some of his great Men were grown Dilirious and Whymsical, that fancy'd Crowns and Kingdoms were to come and go, just as the great Divan at their Court should direct. This confusion of Circumstances has occasion'd a certain Copy of Verses to appear about the Moon, which in our Characters may be read as follows.

Wondelis Idulasin na Perixola Metartos,
Strigunia Crolias Xerin Hytale fylos;
Farnicos Galvare Orpto sonamel Egonsberch,
Sih lona Sipos Gullia Ropta Tylos.

'Which may be English'd thus.

Casar you Trifle with the World in vain,
Think rather now of Germany than Spain;
He's hardly fit to fill th' Eagle's Throne,
Who gives new Crowns, and can't protect his own.

'But after all to come closer to the Point, if I can now make it out that whatever it was before, this very Practice of declaring a second Son to be King of Ebronia, has publickly own'd the Proceedings of the King of Gallunaria to be Just, and the Title of his Grandson to be much better than the Title of the now declar'd King, what shall we call it then?

'In order to this, 'tis first necessary to examine the Title of the present King, and to enter into the history of his coming to the Crown, in which I shall be very Brief.

'The last King of Ebronia dying without Issue, and a former Renunciation taking place, the Succession devolves on the House of the Eagle as before, of whom the present Eagle is the eldest Branch.

'But the late King of Ebronia, to prevent the Succession of the Eagle's Line, makes a Will, and supplies the Proviso of Renunciation by Devising, Giving or Bequeathing the Crown to the Grandson of his Sister.

'The King of Gallunaria insists that this is a lawful Title to the Crown, and seizes it accordingly, inflating his Grandson in the Possession.

'The Eagle alledges the Renunciation to confirm his Title as Heir; and as to the Will of the late King, he says Crowns cannot descend by Gift, and tho' the late King had an undoubted Right to enjoy it himself, he had none to give it away.

'To make the application of this History as short as may be, I demand then what Right has the Eagle to give it to his second Son? if Crowns are not to descend by Gift, he may have a Right to enjoy it, but can have none to give it away, but if he has a Right to give it away; so had the former King, and then the present King has a better Title to it than the new one, because his Gift was Prior to this of the Eagle.

'I would be glad to see this answer'd; and if it can't, then I Query whether the Eagle's Senses ought not to be question'd, for setting up a Title very Foundation for which he quarrels at him that is in Possession, and so confirm the honesty of the Possessor's Title by his own Practice.?

'From the whole, I make no Scruple to say that either the Eagle's second Son has no Title to the Kingdom of Ebronia, or else giving of Crowns is a legal Practice; and if Crowns may descend by Gift, then has the other King a better Title than he, because it was given him first, and the Eagle has only given away what he had no Right to, because 'twas given away before he had any Title to it himself.

'Further, the Posterity of the Eagle's eldest Son are manifestly injur'd in this Action, for Kings can no more give away their Crowns from their Posterity, than from themselves; if the Right be in the Eagle, 'tis his, as he's the eldest Male Branch of the House of the great Lip, not as he is Eagle, and from him the Crown of Ebronia by the same Right of Devolution descends to his Posterity, and rests on the Male Line of every eldest Branch. If so, no Act of Renunciation can alter this Succession, for that is a Gift, and the Gift is exploded, or else the whole House of the great Lip is excluded; so that let the Argument be turn'd and twisted never so many ways, it all Centers in this, that the present Person can have no Title to the Crown of Ebronia.

'If he has any Title, 'tis from the Gift of his Father and elder Brother; if the Gift of a Crown is no good Title, then his Title cannot be good; If the Gift of a Crown is a good Title, then the Crown was given away before, and so neither he nor his Father has any Title.

'Let him that can answer these Paradoxes defend his Title if he can; and what shall we now say to the War in Ebronia, only this, that they are going to fight for the Crown of Ebronia? and to take it away from one that has no Right to it, to give it to one that has a less Right than he, and 'tis to be fear'd that if Heaven be Righteous, 'twill succeed accordingly.

'The Gentlemen of Letters who have wrote of this in our Lunar World, on the Subject of the Gallunarians Title, have took a great deal of Liberty in the Eagle's behalf, to Banter and Ridicule the Gallunarian sham of a Title, as if it were a pretence too weak for any Prince to make use of, to talk of Kings giving their Crowns by Will.

Kingdoms and Governments, says a Learned Lunar author, are not things of such indifferent Value to be given away, like a Token left for a Legacy. If any Prince has ever given or transferr'd his Government, it has been done by solemn Act, and the People have been call'd to assent and confirm such Concessions.

'Then the same Author goes on, to Treat the King of Gallunaria with a great deal of Severity, and exposes his Politicks, that he should think to put upon the Moon with so empty, so weak, so ridiculous a Pretence, as the Will of a weak Headed Prince, who neither had a Right to give his Crown, nor a Brain to know what he was doing, and he laughs to think what the King of Gallunaria would have said to have such a dull Trick as that, put upon him in any such Case.

'Now when we have been so Witty upon this very Article, of giving away the Crown to the King of Gallunaria's Grandson, as an incongruous and ridiculous Thing, shall we come to make the same Incongruity be the Foundation of a War?

'With what Justice can we make a War for a Prince who has only a good Title, by Vertue of the self same Action which makes the Grandson of his Enemy have a bad Title.

'I always thought we had a Just Ground to make War on Ebronia, as we were bound by former Alliances to assist the Eagle in the recovery of it in case of the death of the late King of that Country.

'But now the Eagle has refus'd the Succession, and his Eldest Son has refus'd it, I would be glad to see it prov'd how the second Son can have a Title, and yet the other King have no Title.

'What a strange sort of a Thing is the Crown of Ebronia, that two of the greatest Princes of the Lunar World should Fight, not who shall have it, for neither of them will accept of it, but who shall have the Power of giving it away.

'Here are four Princes refuse it; the King of Gallunaria's Sons had a Title in Right of their Mother, and 'twas not the former Renunciations that would have barr'd them, if this softer way had not been found out; for time was it has been pleaded on behalf of the eldest Son of the Gallunarian King, that his Mother could not give away his Right before he was born.

'Then the Eagle has a Right, and under him his eldest Son; and none of all these four will accept of the Crown; I believe all the Moon can't find four more that would refuse it.

'Now, tho' none of these think it worth accepting themselves, yet they fall out about the Right of giving it away. The King of Gallunaria will not accept of it himself, but he gets a Gift from the last Incumbent. This, says the Eagle, can't be a good Title, for the late King had no Right to make a Deed of Gift of the Crown, since a King is only Tennant for Life, and Succession of Crowns either must descend by a Lineal Progression in the Right of Primogeniture, or else they lose the Tenure, and devolve on the People.

'Now as this Argument holds good the Eagle has an undoubted Title to the Crown of Ebronia: But then, says his Eaglish Majesty, I cannot accept of the Crown my self for I am the Eagle, and my eldest Son has two Kingdoms already, and is in a fair way to be Eagle after me, and 'tis not worth while for him, but I have a second Son, and we will give it him.

'Now may the King of Gallunaria say, if one Gift is good, another is good, and ours is the first Gift, and therefore we will keep it; and tho' I solemnly declare I should be very sorry to see the Crown of Ebronia rest in the House of the Gallunarian, because our Trade will suffer exceedingly; yet if never so much damage were to come of it, we ought to do Justice in the World; if neither the Eagle nor his eldest Son will be

King of Ebronia, but a Deed of Gift shall be made, the first Gift has the Right, for nothing can be given away to two People at once, and 'tis apparent that the late King had as much Right to give it away as any Body.

'The poor Ebronians are in a fine Condition all this while, that no Body concerns them in the Matter; neither Party has so much as thought it worth while to ask them who they would have to Reign over them, here has been no Assembly, no Cortez, no Meeting of the People of Ebronia, neither Collectively or Representatively, no general Convention of the Nobility, no House of Feathers, but Ebronia lies as the spoil of the Victor wholly passive, and her People and Princes, as if they were wholly unconcern'd, lie by and look on, whoever is like to be King, they are like to suffer deeply by the Strife, and yet neither side has thought fit to consult them about it.

'The conclusion of the whole Matter is in short this, here is certainly a false Step taken, how it shall be rectify'd is not the present Business, nor am I Wise enough to Prescribe. One Man may do in a Moment what all the Lunar World cannot undo in an Age. 'Tis not be thought the Eagle will be prevail'd on to undo it, nay he has Sworn not to alter it.

'I am not concern'd to prove the Title of the present King of Ebronia, no, nor of the Eagles neither; but I think I can never be answer'd in this, that this Gift of the Eagles to his second Son is preposterous, inconsistent with all his Claim to the Crown, and the greatest confirmation of the Title of his Enemy that it was possible to give, and no doubt the Gallunarians will lay hold of the Argument.

'If this Prince was the Eagle's eldest Son, he might have a Just Right from the concession of his Father, because the Right being inherent, he only receiv'd from him an Investiture of Time, but as this young Gentleman is a second Son he has no more Right, his elder Brother being alive, than your Grand Seignior, or Czar of Muscovy in your World.

'Let them Fight then for such a Cause, who valuing only the Pay, make War a Trade, and Fight for any thing they are bid to Fight for, and as such value not the Justice of the War, nor trouble their Heads about Causes and Consequences, so they have their Pay, 'tis well enough for them.

'But were the Justice of the War examin'd, I can see none, this Declaring a new King who has no Right but by a Gift, and pulling down one that had it by a Gift before, has so much Contradiction in it, that I am afraid no Wise Man, or Honest Man will embark in it.

Your
Humble Servant,
The Man in the Moon.

I wou'd have no Body now pretend to scandalize the Writer of this Letter, which being for the Gallunarians, for no Man in the Moon had more Aversion for them than he, but he would have had the War carry'd on upon a right Bottom, Justice and Honesty regarded in it, and as he said often, they had no need to go out of the Road of Justice, for had they made War in the great Eagle's Name all had been well.

Nor was he a false Prophet, for as this was ill grounded, so it was as ill carry'd on, met with Shocks,

Rubs and Disappointments every way. The very first Voyage the new King made, he had like to ha' been drown'd by a very violent Tempest, things not very usual in those Countries; and all the Progress that had been made in his behalf when I came away from that Lunar World, had not brought him so much as to be able to set his Foot upon his new Kingdom of Ebronia, but his Adversary by wonderful Dexterity, and the Assistance of his old Grandfather the Gallunarian Monarch, beat his Troops upon all Occasions, invaded his Ally that pretended to assist him, and kept a quiet Possession of all the vast Ebronian Monarchy; and but at last by the powerful Diversion of the Solunarian Fleet, a Shock was given them on another Side, which if it had not happen'd, it was thought the new King had been sent home again Re Infecta.

Being very much Shockt in my Judgment of this Affair, by these unanswerable Reasons; I enquir'd of my Author who were the Directors of this Matter? he told me plainly it was done by those great States Men, which the Solunarian Queen had lately very Justly turn'd out, whose Politicks were very unaccountable in a great many other things, as well as in that.

'Tis true, the War was carry'd on under the new Ministry, and no War in the World can be Juster, on account of the Injustice and Encroachment of the Gallunarian Monarch.

The Queen therefore and her present Ministers, go on with the War on Principles of Confederacy; 'tis the business of the Solunarians to beat the Invader out, and then let the People come and make a fair Decision who they will have to Reign over them.

This indeed justifies the War in Ebronia to be Right, but for the Personal Proceedure as before, 'tis all Contradiction and can never be answer'd.

I hope no Man will be so malicious, as to say I am hereby reflecting on our War with Spain. I am very forward to say, it is a most Just and Reasonable War, as to paralels between the Case of the Princes, in defending the Matter of Personal Right, Hic labor, Hoc opus.

Thus however you see Humanum eft Errare, whether in this World or in the Moon, 'tis all one, Infallibility of Councels any more than of Doctrine, is not in Man.

The Reader may observe, I have formerly noted there was a new Consolidator to be Built, and observ'd what struggle there was in the Moon about choosing the Feathers.

I cannot omit some further Remarks here, as

1. It is to be observ'd, that this last Consolidator was in a manner quite worn out. - It had indeed continu'd but 3 Year, which was the stated Time by Law, but it had been so Hurry'd, so Party Rid, so often had been up in the Moon, and made so many such extravagant Flights, and unnecessary Voyages thither, that it began to be exceedingly worn and defective.

2. This occasion'd that the light fluttering Feathers, and the fermented Feathers made strange Work of it; nay, sometimes they were so hot, they were like to ha' ruin'd the whole Fabrick, and had it not been for the great Feather in the Center, and a few Negative Feathers who were Wiser than the rest, all the

Machines had been broke to pieces, and the whole Nation put into a most strange Confusion.

Sometimes their Motion was so violent an precipitant, that there was great apprehensions of its being set on Fire by its own Velocity, for swiftness of Motion is allow'd by the Sages and so so's to produce Fire as in Wheels, Mills and several sorts of Mechanick Engines which are frequently Fir'd, and so in Thoughts, Brains, Assemblies, Consolidators, and all such combustible Things.

Indeed these things were of great Consequence, and therefore require some more nice Examination than ordinary, and the following Story will in part explain it.

Among the rest of the Broils they had with the Grandees, one happen'd on this occasion.

One of the Tacking Feathers being accidentally met by a Grandee's Footman, whom it seems wanted some Manners, the Slave began to haloo him in the Street, with a Tacker, a Tacker, a Feather-Fool, a Tacker, &c. and so brought the Mob about him, and had not the Grandee himself come in the very interim, and rescu'd the Feather, the Mob had demolisht him, they were so enrag'd.

As this Gentleman-Feather was rescu'd with great Courtesie by the Grandee, taken into his Coach and carry'd home to his House, he desir'd to speak with the Footman.

The Fellow being call'd in, was ask't by him who employ'd him, or set him on to offer him this Insult?

the Footman being a ready bold Fellow, told him no Body Sir, but you are all grown so ridiculous to the whole Nation, that if the 134 of you were left but to us Footmen, and it was not in more respect to our Masters, than you, we should Cure you of ever coming into the Consolidator again, and all the People in the Moon are of our Mind.

But says the Feather, why do you call me Fool too? why Sir, says he, because no Body could ever tell us what it was you drove at, and we ha' been told you never knew your selves; now if one of you Tacking Feathers would but tell the World what your real Design was, they would be satisfy'd, but to be leaders in the Consolidator, and to Act without Meaning, without Thought or Design, must argue your' Fools, or worse, and you will find all the Moon of my Mind.

But what if we had a meaning, says the Feather-Man? why then, says the Footman, we shall leave calling you Fools, and call you Knaves, for it could never be an Honest one, so that you had better stand as you do: and I make it out thus.

You knew, that upon your Tacking the Crolians to the Tribute Bill, the Grandees must reject both, they having declar'd against reading any Bills Tackt together, as being against their Priviledges. Now if you had any Design, it must be to have the Bill of Tribute lost, and that must be to disappoint all the publick Affairs, expose the Queen, break all Measures, discourage the Confederates, and putting all things backward, bring the Gallunarian Forces upon them, and put all Solunaria into Confusion. Now Sir, says he, we cannot have such course Thoughts of you, as to believe you could design such dark, mischievous things as these, and therefore we chose to believe you all Fools, and not fit to be put into a Consolidator again; than Knaves and Traytors to your Country, and consequently fit for a worse Place.

The plainness of the Footman was such, and so unanswerable, that his Master was fain to check him, and so the Discourse broke off, and we shall leave it there, and proceed to the Story.

The Men of the Feather as I have noted, who are represented here by the Consolidator, fell all together by the Ears, and all the Moon was in a combustion. The Case was as follows.

They had three times lost their quallifying Law, and particularly they observ'd the Grandees were the Men that threw it out, and notwithstanding the Plot of the Tackers, as they call'd them, who were as I noted, observ'd to be in Conjunction with the Crolians, yet the Law always past the Feathers, but still the Grandees quasht it.

To show their Resentment at the Grandees, they had often made attempts to mortify them, sometimes Arraigning them in general, sometimes Impeaching private Members of their House, but still all wou'd not do, the Grandees had the better of them, and going on with Regularity and Temper, the Consolidators or Feather-Men always had the worst, the Grandees had the applause of all the Moon, had the last Blow on every Occasion, and the other sunk in their Reputation exceedingly.

It is necessary to understand here, that the Men of the Feather serve in several Capacities, and under several

Denominations, and act by themselves, singly consider'd, they are call'd the Consolidator, and the Feathers we mention'd abstracted from their Persons, make the glorious Engine we speak of, and in which, when any suddain Motion takes them, they can all shut themselves up, and away for the Moon.

But when these are joyn'd with the Grandees, and the Queen, so United, they make a great Cortez, or general Collection of all the Governing Authority of the Nation.

When this last Fraction happen'd, the Men of the Feather were under an exceeding Ferment, they had in some Passion taken into their Custody, some good Honest Lunar Country-Men, for an Offence, which indeed few but themselves ever immagin'd was a Crime, for the poor Men did nothing but pursue their own Right by the Law.

'Tis thought the Men of the Feather soon saw they were in the Wrong, but acted like some Men in our World, that when they make a mistake, being too Proud to own themselves in the wrong, run themselves into worse Errors to mend it.

So these Lunar Gentlemen disdaining to have it said they could be mistaken, committed two Errors to conceal one, 'till at last they came to be laught at by all the Moon.

These poor Men having lain a long while in Prison, for little or no Crime, at last were advis'd to apply themselves to the Law for Discharge; the Law would fairly have Discharg'd them; for in that Country, no Man may be Imprison'd, but he must in a certain Time be Tryed, or let go upon pledges of his Friends, much like our giving Bail on a Writ of Habeas Corpus; but the Judges, whether over-aw'd by the Feathers, or what was the Cause, Authors have not determin'd, did not care to venture Discharging them.

The poor Men thus remanded, apply'd themselves to the Grandees who were then Sitting, and who are the Soveraign Judicature of the Country, and before whom Appeals lie from all Courts of Justice. The Grandees as in Duty bound, appear'd ready to do them Justice, but the Queen was to be apply'd to, first to grant a Writ, or a Warrant for a Writ, call'd in their Country a Writ of Follies, which is as much as to say Mistakes.

The Consolidators foreseeing the Consequence, immediately apply'd themselves to the Queen with an Address, the Terms of which were so Undu - l and Unman - ly, that had she not been a Queen of unusual Candor and Goodness, she would have Treated them as they deserv'd, for they upbraided her with their Freedom and Readiness in granting her Supplies, and therefore as good as told her they expected she should do as they desir'd.

These People that knew the Supplies given, were from necessity, Legal, and for their own Defence, while the granting their Request, must have been Illegal, Arbitrary, a Dispensing with the Laws, and denying Justice to her Subjects, the very thing they ruin'd her Father for, were justly provok'd to see their good Queen so barbarously Treated.

The Queen full of Goodness and Calmness, gave them a gentle kind Answer, but told them she must be careful to Act with due Regard to the Laws, and could not interrupt the course of Judicial Proceedings; and at the same time granted the Writ, having first consulted with her Council, and receiv'd the Opinion of all the Judges, that it was not only Safe, but Just and Reasonable, and a Right to her People which she could not deny.

This Proceeding gall'd the Feathers to the quick, and finding the Grandees resolv'd to proceed Judicially upon the said Writ of Follies, which if they did, the Prisoners would be deliver'd and the Follies fixt upon the Feathers, they sent their Poursuivants took them out of the Common Prison, and convey'd them separately and privately into Prisons of their own.

This rash and unprecedented Proceedings, pusht them farther into a Labrinth, from whence it was impossible they could ever find their way out, but with infinite Loss to their Reputation, like a Sheep in a thick Wood, that at every Briar pulls some of the Wool from her Back, till she comes out in a most scandalous Pickle of Nakedness and Scratches.

The Grandees immediately publisht six Articles in Vindication of the Peoples Right, against the assum'd Priviledges of the Feathers, the Abstract of which is as follows.

1. That the Feathers had no Right to Claim, or make any new Priviledges for themselves, other than they had before.

2. That every Freeman of the Moon had a Right to repel Injury with Law.

3. That Imprisoning the 5 Countrymen by the Feathers,

was assuming a new Priviledge they had no Right to, and a subjecting the Subjects Right to their Arbitrary Votes.

4. That a Writ of Deliverance, or removing the Body, is the legal Right of every Subject in the Moon, in order to his Liberty, in case of Imprisonment.

5. That to punish any Person for assisting the Subjects, in procuring or prosecuting the said Writ of Deliverance, is a breach of the Laws, and a thing of dangerous Consequence.

6. That a Writ of Follies is not a Grace, but a Right, and ought not to be deny'd to the Subject.

These Resolves struck the languishing Reputation of the Feathers with the dead Palsie, and they began to stink in the Nostrils of all the Nations in the Moon.

But besides this, they had one strange effect, which was a prodigious disappointment to the Men of the Feather.

I had observ'd before, that there was to be a new Set of Feathers, provided in order to Building another Consolidator, according to a late Law for a new Engine every three Years. Now several of these Men of the Feather, who thought their Feathers capable of serving again, had made great Interest, and been at great Cost to have their old Feathers chosen again, but the People had entertain'd such scoundrel Opinions of these Proceedings, such as Tacking, Consolidating, Imprisoning Electors, Impeaching without Tryal, Writs of Follies and the like, that if any one was known to be concern'd in any of these things, no Body would Vote for him.

The Gentlemen were so mortify'd at this, that even the hottest High-Church Solunarian of them all, if he put in any where to be re-chosen, the first thing he had to do, was to assure the People he was no Tacker, none of the 134, and a vast deal of difficulty they had to Purge themselves of this blessed Action, which they us'd to value themselves on before, as their Glory and Merit.

Thus they grew asham'd of it as a Crime, got Men to go about to vouch for them to the Country People, that they were no Tackers, nay, one of them to clear himself loudly forswore it, and taking a Glass of Wine wisht it might never pass thro' him, if he was a Tacker, tho' all Men suspected him to be of that Number too, he having been one of the forwardest that way on all Occasions, of any Person among the South Folk of the Moon.

In like manner, one of the Feathers for the middle Province of the Country, who us'd to think it his Honour to be for the qualifying Law, seeing which way the humour of the Country ran, took as much Pains now to tell the People he was no Tacker, as he did before, to promise them that he would do his utmost to have the Crolians reduc'd, and that Bill to pass, the Reason of which was plain, that he saw if it should be known he was a Tacker, he should never have his Feather return'd to be put into the Consolidator.

The Heats and Feuds that the Feathers and the Grandees were now run into, began to make the latter very uneasie, and they sent to the Grandees to hasten them, and put them in mind of passing some Laws they had sent up to them for raising Mony, and which lay before them, knowing that as soon as those Laws were past, the Queen would break 'em up, and they being very willing to be gone, before these things came too far upon the Stage, urg'd them to dispatch.

But the Grandees resolving to go thoro' with the Matter, sent to them to come to a Treaty on the foot of the six Articles, and to bring any Reasons they could, to prove the Power they had to Act as they had done with the Country-men, and with the Lawyers they had put in Prison for assisting them.

The Feathers were very backward and stiff about this Conference, or Treaty, 'till at last the Grandees having sufficiently expos'd them to all the Nation, the Bills were past, the Grandees caus'd the particulars to be Printed, and a Representation of their Proceedings, and the Feathers foul Dealings to the Queen of the Country, and so her Majesty sent them Home.

But if they were asham'd of being call'd Tackers before, they were doubly mortify'd at this now, nay the Country resented it so exceedingly, that some of them began to consider whether they should venture to go Home or no; Printed Lists of their Names were Publish'd, tho' we do not say they were true Lists, for it was a hard thing to know which were true Lists, and which were not, nor indeed could a true List be made, no Man being able to retain the exact Account of who were the Men in his Memory.

For as there were 134 Tackers, so there were 141 of these, who by a Name of Distinction, were call'd Lebusyraneim, in English Ailesbury-men.

The People were so exasperated against these, that they express'd their Resentment upon all Occasions, and least the Queen should think that the Nation approv'd the Proceedings, they drew up a Representation or Complaint, full of most dutiful Expressions to their Queen, and full of Resentment against the Feathers, the Copy of which being handed about the Moon the last time I was there, I shall take the Pains to put it into English in the best manner I can, keeping as near the Originial as possible.

If any Man shall now wickedly suggest, that this Relation has any retrospect to the Affairs of England, the Author declares them malitious Misconstruers of his honest Relation of Matters from this remote Country, and offers his positive Oath for their Satisfaction, that the very last Journy he made into those Lunar Regions, this Matter was upon the Stage, of which, if this Treatise was not so near its conclusion, the Reader might expect a more particular Account.

If there is any Analogy or similitude between the Transactions of either World, he cannot account for that, 'tis application makes the Ass.

And yet sometimes he has thought, as some People Fable of the Platonick Year, that after such a certain Revolution of Time, all Things are Transacted over again, and the same People live again, are the fame Fools, Knaves, Philosophers and Mad-men they were before, tho' without any Knowledge of, or Retrospect to what they acted before; so why should it be impossible, that as the Moon and this World are noted before to be Twins and Sisters, equal in Motion and in Influence, and perhaps in Qualities, the same secret

Power should so act them, as that like Actions and Circumstances should happen in all Parts of both Worlds at the same time.

I leave this Thought to the improvement of our Royal Learned Societies of the Anticacofanums, Opposotians, Periodicarians, Antepredestinarians, Universal Soulians, and such like unfathomable People, who, without question, upon mature Enquiry will find out the Truth of this Matter.

But if any one shall scruple the Matter of Fact as I have here related it, I freely give him leave to do as I did, and go up to the Moon for a Demonstration; and if upon his return he does not give ample Testimony to the Case in every part of it, as here related, I am content to pass for the Contriver of it my self, and be punish'd as the Law shall say I deserve.

Nor was this all the publick Matters, in which this Nation of Solunarians took wrong Measures, for about this time, the Misunderstandings between the Southern and Northern Men began again, and the Solunarians made several Laws, as they call'd them, to secure themselves against the Dangers they pretended might accrue from the new Measures the Nolunarians had taken; but so unhappily were they blinded by the strife among themselves, and by-set by Opinion and Interest, that every Law they made, or so much as attempted to make, was really to the Advantage, and to the Interest of the Northern-Men, and to their own loss; so Ignorantly and Weak-headed was these High Solunarian Church-Men in the true Interest of their Country, led by their implacable Malice at Crolianism, which as is before noted, was the Establisht Religion of that Country.

But as this Matter was but Transacting when I took the other Remarks, and that I did not obtain a full Understanding of it, 'till my second Voyage, I refer it to a more full Relation of my farther Travels that way, when I shall not fail to give a clear State of the Debate of the two Kingdoms, in which the Southern Men had the least Reason, and the worst Success that ever they had in any Affair of that Nature for many Years before.

It was always my Opinion in Affairs on this side the Moon, that tho' sometimes a foolish Bolt may hit the Point, and a random Shot kill the Enemy, yet that generally Discretion and Prudence of Mannagement, had the Advantage, and met with a proportion'd Success, find things were, or were not happy, in their Conclusion as they were, more or less wisely Contriv'd and Directed.

And tho' it may not be allow'd to be so here, yet I found it more constantly so there, Effects were true to their Causes, and confusion of Councils never fail'd in the Moon to be follow'd by distracted and destructive Consequences.

This appear'd more eminently in the Dispute between these two Lunar Nations we are speaking of; never were People in the Moon, whatever they might be in other Places, so divided in their Opinions about a matter of such Consequence. Some were for declaring War immediately upon the Northern Men, tho' they could show no Reason at all why, only because they would not do as they would have 'em; a parcel of poor Scoundrel, Scabby Rogues, they ought to be made submit, what! won't they declare the same King as we do! hang them Rogues! a pack of Crolian Prestarian Devils, we must make them do it, down with them the shortest Way, declare War immediately, and down with them. - Nay some were for falling on them directly, without the formality of declaring War.

Others, more afraid than hurt, cry'd out Invasions, Depredation, Fire and Sword, the Northern Men would be upon them immediately, and propos'd to Fortify their Frontiers, and file off their Forces to the Borders; nay, so apprehensive did those Men of Prudence pretend to be, that they order'd Towns to be Fortify'd 100 Mile off of the Place, when all this while the poor Northern Men did nothing but tell them, that unless they would come to Terms, they would not have the same King as they, and they took some Measures to let them see they did not purpose to be forc'd to it.

Another sort of Wiser Men than these, propos'd to Unite with them, hear their Reasons, and do them Right. These indeed were the only Men that were in the right Method of concluding this unhappy Broil, and for that Reason, were the most unlikely to succeed.

But the Wildest Notion of all, was, when some of the Grandees made a grave Address to the Queen of the Country, to desire the Northern Men to settle Matters first, and to tell them, that when that was done, they should see what these would do for them. This was a home Stroke, if it had but hit, and the Misfortune only lay in this, That the Northern Men were not Fools enough; the clearness of the Air in those cold Climates generally clearing the Head so early, that those People see much farther into a Mill-stone than any Blind Man in all the Southern Nations of the Moon.

There was an another unhappiness in this Case, which made the Matter yet more confus'd, and that was, that the Souldiers had generally no gust to this War. - This was an odd Case; for those sort of Gentlemen, especially in the World in the Moon, don't use to enquire into the Justice of the Case they Fight for, but they reckon 'tis their Business to go where they are sent, and kill any Body they are order'd to kill, leaving their Governors to answer for the Justice of it; but there was another Reason to be given why the Men of the Sword were so averse, and always talk't coldly of the fighting Part, and tho' the Northern Men call'd it fear, yet I cannot joyn with them in that, for to fear requires Thinking; and some of our Solunarians are absolutely protected from the first, because they never meddle with the last, except when they come to the Engine, and therefore 'tis plain it could not proceed from Fear.

It has puzzl'd the most discerning Heads of the Age, to give a Reason from whence this Aversion proceeded, and various Judgments have been given of it.

The Nolunarians jested with them, and when they talk't of Fighting, bad them look back into History, and examine what they ever made of a Nolunarian War, and whether they had not been often well beaten, and sent short home, bid them have a care of catching a Tartar, as we call it, and always made themselves merry with it.

They banter'd the Solunarians too, about the Fears and Terrors they were under, from their Arming themselves, and putting themselves in a posture of Defence, - When it was easy to see by the nature of the thing, that their Design was not a War, but a Union upon just Conditions, that it was a plain Token that they design'd either to put some affront upon the

Nolunarians, to deny them some just Claims, or to impose something very Provoking upon them more than they had yet done, that they were so exceeding fearful of an Invasion from them.

Tho' these were sufficient to pass for Reasons in other Cases, yet it could not be so here, but I saw there must be something else in it. As I was thus wondering at this unusual backwardness of the Souldiers, I enquir'd a little farther into the meaning of it, and quickly found the Reason was plain, there was nothing to be got by it, that People were Brave, Desperate and Poor, the Country Barren, Mountainous and Empty, so that in short there would be nothing but Blows, and Souldiers Fellows to be had, and I always observ'd that Souldiers never care to be knockt on the Head, and get nothing by the Bargain.

In short, I saw plainly the Reasons that prompted the Solunarians to Insult their Neighbours of the North, were more deriv'd from the regret at their Establishing Crolianism, than at any real Causes they had given, or indeed were in a condition to give them.

These, and abundance more particular Observations I made, but as I left the thing still in agitation, and undetermin'd, I shall refer it to another Voyage which I purpose to make thither, and at my return, may perhaps set that Case in a clearer Light than our Sight can yet bear to look at it in.

If in my second Vovage I should undeceive People in the Notions they entertain'd of those Northern People, and convince them that the Solunarians were really the Aggressors, and had put great hardships upon them, I might possibly do a Work, that if it met with

Encouragement, might bring the Solunarians to do them Justice, and that would set all to Rights, the two Nations might easily become one, and Unite for ever, or at least become Friends, and give mutual Assistance to each other; and I cannot but own such an Agreement would make them both very formidable, but this I refer to another time. -

At the same time I cannot leave it without a Remark that this Jealousy between the two Nations, may perhaps in future Ages be necessary to be maintain'd, in order to find some better Reasons for Fortifications, Standing Armies, Guards and Garisons than could be given in the Reign of the great Prince I speak of, the Queen's Predecessor, tho' his was against Forreign insulting Enemy.

But the Temper of the Solunarian High Party was always such, that they would with much more case give thanks for a Standing Army against the Nolunarians and Crolians, than agree to one Legion against the Abrogratzians and Gallunarians.

But of these Things I am also promis'd a more particular Account upon my Journy into that Country.

I cannot however conclude this Matter, without giving some Account of my private Observations, upon what was farther to be seen in this Country.

And had not my Remarks on their State Matters taken up more of my Thoughts than I expected, I might have entred a little upon their other Affairs, such as their Companies, their Commerce, their Publick Offices, their Stock-Jobbers, their Temper, their Conversation, their Women, their Stages, Universities, their

Courtiers, their Clergy, and the Characters of the severals under all these Denominations, but these must be referr'd to time, and my more perfect Observations.

But I cannot omit, that tho' I have very little Knowledge of Books, and had obtain'd less upon their Language, yet I could not but be very inquisitive after their Libraries and Men of Letters.

Among their Libraries I found not abundance of their own Books, their Learning having so much of Demonstration, and being very Hieroglyphical, but I found to my great Admiration vast quantities of Translated Books out of all Languages of our World.

As I thought my self one of the first, at least of our Nation, that ever came thus far; it was, you may be sure no small surprize to me to find all the most valluable parts of Modern Learning, especially of Politicks, Translated from our Tongue, into the Lunar Dialect, and stor'd up in their Libraries with the Remarks, Notes and Observations of the Learned Men of that Climate upon the Subject.

Here, among a vast croud of French Authors condemn'd in this polite World for trifling, came a huge Volume containing, Les Oevres de scavans, which has 19 small Bells painted upon the Book of several disproportion'd sizes.

I enquir'd the meaning of that Hieroglyphick, which the Master of the Books told me, was to signify that the substance was all Jingle and Noise, and that of 30 Volumes which that one Book contains, 29 of them have neither Substance, Musick, Harmony nor value in them.

The History of the Fulsoms, or a Collection of 300 fine Speeches made in the French Accademy at Paris, and 1500 gay Flourishes out of Monsieur Boileau, all in Praise of the invincible Monarch of France.

The Duke of Bavaria's Manifesto, shewing the Right of making War against our Sovereigns, from whence the People of that Lunar World have noted that the same Reasons which made it lawful to him to attempt the Imperial Power, entitle him to lose his own, viz. Conquest, and the longest Sword.

Jack a both Sides, or a Dialogue between Pasquin and Marforio, upon the Subject Matter of the Pope's sincerity in Case of the War in Italy. Written by a Citizen of Ferrara. One side arguing upon the occasion of the Pope's General wheedling the Imperialists to quit that Country. The other bantering Imperial Policy, or the Germains pretending they were Trickt out of Italy, when they could stay there no longer.

Lewis the Invincible, by Monsieur Boileau. A Poem, on the Glory of his most Christian Majesties Arms at Hochstedt, and Verue.

All these Translations have innumerable Hyerogliphical Notes, and Emblems painted on them, which pass as Comments, and are readily understood in that Climate. For Example, on the Vol. of Dialogues are two Cardinals washing the Pope's Hands under a Cloud that often bespatters them with Blood, signifying that in spight of all his Pretensions he has a Hand in the Broils of Italy. And before him the Sun setting in a Cloud, and a Blind Ballad-Singer making Sonnets upon the brightness of its Lustre.

The three Kings of Brentford, being some Historical Observations on three mighty Monarchs in our World, whose Heroick Actions may be the Subject of future Ages, being like to do little in this, the King of England, King of Poland, and King of Spain. These are describ'd by a Figure, representing a Castle in the Air, and three Knights pointing at it, but they could not catch.

I omit abundance of very excellent pieces, because remote, as three great Volumes of European Misteries, among the vast varieties of which, and very entertaining, I observ'd but a few, such as these:

1. Why Prince Ragotski will make no Peace with the Emperor. - But more particularly why the Emperor won't make Peace with him.

2. Where the Policy of the King of Sweden lies, to persue the King of Poland, and let the Muscovites ravage and destroy his own Subjects.

3. What the Duke of Bavaria propos'd to himself in declaring for France.

4. Why the Protestants of the Confederacy never reliev'd the Camisars.

5. Why there are no Cowards found in the English Service, but among their Sea Captains.

6. Why the King of Portugal did not take Madrid, why the English did not take Cadiz, and why the Spaniards did not take Gibraltar, viz. because the first were Fools, the second Knaves, and the last Spaniards.

7. What became of all the Silver taken at Vigo.

8. Who will be the next King of Scotland.

9. If England should ever want a King, who would think it worth while to accept of it.

10. What specifick difference can be produc'd between a Knave, a Coward, and a Traytor.

Abundance of these Mysteries are Hieroglyphically describ'd in this ample Collection, and without doubt our great Collection of Annals, and Historical Observations, particularly the Learned Mr. Walker, would make great Improvements there.

But to come nearer home, There, to my great Amasement, I found several new Tracts out of our own Language, which I could hardly have imagin'd it possible should have reacht so far.

As first, sundry Transactions of our Royal Society about Winds, and a valuable Desertation of Dr. B.....'s about Wind in the Brain.

A Discourse of Poisons, by the Learned Dr. M..... with Lunar Notes upon it, wherein it appears that Dr. C....d had more Poison in his Tongue, than all the Adders the Moon have in their Teeth.

Nec Non, or Lawyers Latin turn'd into Lunar Burlesque. The Hyerogliphick was the Queens Mony tost in a Blanket, Dedicated to the Attorney General, and five false Latin Councellors.

Mandamus , as it was Acted at Abb...ton Assizes, by

Mr. So....r General, where the Qu..n had her own So...r against her for a bad Cause, and never a Counsel for her in a good one.

Lunar Reflections, being a List of about 2000 ridiculous Errors in History, palpable Falsities, and scandalous Omissions in Mr. Collier's Geographical Dictionary; with a subsequent Enquiry by way of Appendix, into which are his own, and which he has ignorantly deduc'd from ancient Authors.

Assassination and Killing of Kings, prov'd to be a Church of England Doctrin; humbly Dedicated to the Prince of Wales, by Mr. Collier and Mr. Snat; wherein their Absolving Sir John Friend and Sir William Parkins without Repentance, and while they both own'd and justify'd the Fact, is Vindicated and Defended.

Les Bagatelles, or Brom..ys Travels into Italy, a choice Book, and by great Accident preserv'd from the malitious Design of the Author, who diligently Bought up the whole Impression, for fear they should be seen, as a thing of which this ungrateful Age was not worthy.

Killing no Murther, being an Account of the severe Justice design'd to be inflicted on the barbarous Murtherers of the honest Constable at Bow, but unhappily prevented by my Lord N.....m being turn'd out of his Office.

De modo Belli, or an Account of the best Method of making Conquests and Invasion a la Mode de Port St. Mary, 3 Volumes in 80. Dedicated to Sir Hen. Bell...s.

King Charles the first prov'd a T...t. By Edward Earl of Clarendon, 3 Vol. in Fol. Dedicated to the University of Oxford.

The Bawdy Poets, or new and accurate Editions of Catullus, Propertius, and Tibullus, being the Maidenhead of the new Printing Press at Cambridge, Dedicated by the Editor Mr. Ann...y to the University, and in consideration of which, and some Disorders near Casterton, the University thought him fit to represent them in P......t.

Alms no Charity, or the Skeleton of Sir Humphry Mackworth's Bill for relief of the Poor: Being an excellent new Contrivance to find Employment for all the Poor in the Nation, viz. By setting them at Work, to make all the rest of the People as Poor as themselves.

Synodicum Superlativum, being sixteen large Volumes of the vigorous Proceedings of the English Convocation, digested into Years, one Volume to every Year. - Wherein are several large Lists of the Heretical, Atheistical, Deistical and other pernitious Errors which have been Condemn'd in that Venerable Assembly, the various Services done, and weighty Matters dispatcht, for the Honour of the English Church, for sixteen Years last past, with their formal Proceedings against Asgil, Coward, Toland and others, for reviving old Antiquated Errors in Doctrine, and Publishing them to the World as their own.

New Worlds in Trade, being a vast Collection out of the Journals of the Proceedings of the Right Honourable the Commissioners of Trade, with several Eminent Improvements in general Negoce, vast Schemes of Business, and new Discoveries of

Settlements and Correspondences in Forreign Parts, for the Honour and Advantage of the English Merchants, being 12 Volumes in Fol. and very scarce and valluable Books.

Legal Rebellion, or an Argument proving that all sorts of Insurrections of Subjects against their Princes, are lawful, and to be supported whenever they suit with our Occasions, made good from the Practice of France with the Hungarians, the English with the Camisars, the Swede with the Poles, the Emperor with the Subjects of Naples, and all the Princes of the World as they find occasion, a large Volume in Folio, with a Poem upon the Sacred Right of Kingly Power.

Ignis Fatuus or the Occasional Bill in Minature, a Farce, as it was acted by his Excellency the Lord Gr...il's Servants in Carolina.

Running away the shortest way to Victory, being a large Dissertation, shewing to save the Queens Ships, is the best way to beat the French.

The Tookites, a Poem upon the 134.

A new Tract upon Trade, being a Demonstration that to be always putting the People upon customary Mourning, and wearing Black upon every State Occasion, is an excellent Encouragement to Trade, and a means to employ the Poor.

City Gratitude, being a Poem on the Statue erected by the Court of Aldermen at the upper end of Cheapside, to the Immortal Memory of King William.

There were many more Tracts to be found in this

place; but these may suffice for a Specimen, and to excite all Men that would encrease their Understandings in humane Mysteries, to take a Voyage to this enlightned Country. Where their Memories, thinking Faculties and Penetration, will no question be so Tackt and Consolidated, that when they return, they all Write Memoirs of the Place, and communicate to their Country the Advantages they have reapt by their Voyage, according to the laudable Example of their

Most humble Servant,

The Man in the Moon.

www.ingramcontent.com/pod-product-compliance
Lightning Source LLC
Chambersburg PA
CBHW020551310726
48979CB00008B/1175/J

* 9 7 8 1 4 2 1 8 0 9 2 0 5 *